The Cartel 3:

The Last Chapter

The Cartel 3:

The Last Chapter

Ashley & JaQuavis

www.urbanbooks.net

Urban Books, LLC
78 East Industry Court
Deer Park, NY 11729

ISBN 13: 978-1-60162-257-0
ISBN 10: 1-60162-257-0

First Printing August 2010
Printed in the United States of America

20 19 18 17 16 15 14 13 12

Distributed by Kensington Publishing Corp.
Submit Wholesale Orders to:
Kensington Publishing Corp.
C/O Penguin Group (USA) Inc.
Attention: Order Processing
405 Murray Hill Parkway
East Rutherford, NJ 07073-2316
Phone: 1-800-526-0275
Fax: 1-800-227-9604

Prologue

"We are gathered here today to celebrate the lives of three of God's children."

The preacher stood before the many people who attended the funeral of street royalty. It was a sad day in Miami, and on this day, the streets were like a ghost town. It seemed as if the entire underworld had stopped to commemorate those they had lost. Everyone within the city limits felt this grief. The lives of three street legends had been destroyed, and grief overflowed in the ceremony as three silver-plated coffins sat side by side with an array of flower arrangements around them. It was a bright, sunny day, and it seemed as if God shone his light down from the heavens above to make that hard day seem a tad bit better for the mourning attendees. It was a triple funeral to bury the last of the Diamond family—Breeze, Carter, and Mecca.

The Cartel was no more, and it was the last chapter to what was to be named one of the biggest legacies in Miami's underworld history. Their story was legendary, ruthless . . . and most of all, classic.

Many people were in attendance, but the most important guests were not there to pay their final respects. They were there to confirm that the last of The Cartel was deceased and about to be buried into the ground.

Robin and Aries were in attendance, draped in all-black dresses with big shades on to keep a low profile. Murder also sat beside them. The demise of The Cartel was bittersweet for him, and he gritted his teeth tightly as he thought about Mecca and the missed opportunity to personally kill him on Miamor's behalf. Nevertheless, Mecca was dead, and that would have to be enough for him.

Emilio Estes, Leena, and Monroe Jr. were also in attendance, mourning the loss. They were the only people left alive who could sit in the front pew reserved for family. Although far removed from the Diamond legacy, they were the last of a dying bloodline.

There was an eerie feeling in the air, and everyone there could sense it. As the preacher held the Holy Bible tightly in his hand and read from the book of Psalms, a stretch limo with tinted windows rolled up slowly about fifty yards away from the service. Many people didn't notice it, but the trained eyes were glued to the approaching vehicle.

Emilio Estes looked back and saw the limo pull up, and he watched as it came to a slow stop. Estes knew exactly who it was; it was the crew responsible for the very funeral he was at. Emilio, being in his mid-sixties and not willing to step back into the streets, conceded defeat and pulled his white handkerchief from the top pocket of his suit.

To many, it looked as if Emilio was just removing a hanky, but veterans of the street game knew what that small gesture meant. Emilio wanted the bloodshed to stop, and signaled that he would not retaliate. The war was finally over and The Cartel was no more. Literally, he was waving a white flag. It was officially The Cartel's last chapter.

Chapter One

"Bad girls die slow."
–*Fabian*

The blood in Miamor's eyes blocked out the image of Fabian standing over her, and her shallow, desperate breaths drowned out all sounds in the room. Death loomed over her. She knew it was near. The chill in her lovely bones was every indication that her life was slipping away.

A breathless Fabian stood over her. Her tormentor, her grim reaper leered at her menacingly. The smug grin on his face sickened her as her heart filled with hate for him. It pleased him to watch her die. It was vindication for the hell that she had once put him through, and she knew that the lifestyle she led had ultimately determined the cruel way in which she was about to die. It was the law of nature. She had taken more lives than she could count, had destroyed too many families to remember, and her heart had turned cold so long ago that she did not even care. Now it was her turn. This was her fate, her karma, and because she had pushed away everyone who had ever cared for her, no one would even know that she had disappeared from the face of the earth.

Most people in her position would repent. They would beg for their lives, or feel regret for all of the events that had led up to this torturous moment, but Miamor was not most people. Her hard shell had not cracked, and even under the most gruesome pressure, she still had to maintain some form of control.

Fabian wanted to see her break down. He had done everything that was physically possible to get her to give in. Her face was badly disfigured, her fingernails pulled from their nail beds, and her bones crushed and broken, but still not one tear had fallen. She had passed out many times, but that was a physical response to the pain. Crying was controlled by her mental state, and that was one resolve that was too strong for anyone to conquer.

"Bitch, you're going to beg me for your life," he seethed as he circled her, sweaty from his ruthless assault on her. He lifted his hand and backhanded her with the butt of his gun, causing her neck to snap violently to the right.

Miamor bit her tongue to avoid screaming out in agony. She wouldn't give him the satisfaction of seeing her so weak. Blood poured from her mouth, but it only mixed in with the rest of the blood that soaked her battered body.

He had been in the basement for a full twenty-four hours, killing her slowly, but no matter how hard he tried, he couldn't feel the satisfaction of revenge that he sought. There was something about the look in her eyes that said "fuck you," and even in her most fragile state, her mentality never failed her.

Murder was bred deep within her. Fabian was committing the act of murder, but Miamor was a killer. She breathed murder. It was all she knew, the only thing that she had ever been good at. It was her profession. So, even as she sat in the damp basement, her soul slowly abandoning her, her dainty wrists tightly bound to a wooden chair, her eyes still told the story of the greatest bitch who had ever done it. She was merciless, and even death couldn't wipe her off the map.

There was no escaping this. Her time had come, and Miamor had no regrets. She was on her way to hell, but it was worth the legacy she was leaving behind. Yes, her lifestyle had led her to nothing but loneliness and misery. She had loved two men in her lifetime, but never truly had room in her world for either of them. They would have never understood how she lived or the things that she had been through, and because of this, she had never fully given her heart to another. She had given up so much in order to reign terror in the streets, and to her, it was worth it. If she had chosen to play wifey to men like Murder or Carter, people would have forgotten an ordinary young woman named Miamor; she would have been lost in their shadows. So, she had chosen something much greater. She had chosen the life of murder-for-hire, and now, even after her death, her name would resound loudly in the streets. Her small feet would leave huge shoes to fill in the game. Legend of her notorious wrecking crew, the Murder Mamas, would ring true for years to come. She had made sure that no one would ever forget. Every new hustler coming up in the game would eventually hear the story of Miamor, and now she would forever be notorious.

The sound of the basement door opening and the heavy thud of boots descending the staircase announced a new presence in the room, causing Miamor to lift her head weakly. Anxiety made her heart gallop as she watched a cool, calm, and freshly dressed Mecca saunter down the stairs. A machete hung from his hand.

"Damn, nigga, you ain't done killing this bitch yet? This shit make your dick hard?" Mecca cracked, knowing that an erection would never be possible for Fabian again, thanks to Miamor.

"I wanted this bitch to hurt like I hurt. Bad girls die slow," Fabian stated. "I just want to hear this bitch scream before I kill her."

Mecca's eyes opened wide in surprise as he looked around

the room at the carnage that Fabian's torture had produced. "You done used every trick in the book and you still can't make the bitch holler?"

"Bitch ain't human, fam," Fabian replied.

Mecca chuckled mockingly as he shook his head. "You really are a bitch-ass nigga," he mumbled as he approached Miamor, the blade of the machete screeching across the floor as he dragged it.

Miamor knew that the time for games was over. Mecca had not come back for nothing. He was there to end this, and there was no doubt in her mind that he would. He was the only nigga she had ever met whose murder game matched her own. Mecca would not hesitate. He would kill her without second guessing it. She knew this because if the shoe were on the other foot, he would already be a distant memory.

The faces of everyone she had ever loved flashed before her eyes. She closed them and welcomed the images: Murder, Anisa, Robyn, and Aries. They were all a part of her final fleeting thoughts, but the face the stuck out the most, the last person she thought of, was Carter Jones, the love of her life. He was the man who had showed her a love so strong, one that she knew she would have never been able to fully return. As much as she loved him, she did not deserve him, and he did not deserve the tyranny that she had brought into his life.

She had played a cat and mouse game with Mecca for too long; now it was time for the charade to end. The scent of Mecca's Issey Miyake cologne invaded her senses as he bent down near her ear.

Miamor's eyes remained closed as Mecca took in the image of her. Seeing her this way was poetic for him, a beautiful demise for an ugly situation. The two of them could never co-exist. Her day of reckoning had come.

"My man here feels like you owe him something. Now, I

have a proposition for you. I think you've learned your lesson. I'm not usually a forgiving man, but if you apologize to Fabian here and you admit that you can't fuck with me, then I won't kill you. I'll let you go, as long as you leave Miami . . . my city," Mecca whispered in her ear. He wasn't a nice guy and didn't even imitate one well. He knew that he would never let Miamor live, but he wanted to hear her apologize, and he wanted to hear her admit that that she was beneath him . . . that he held the power . . . that only he could determine whether she lived or died.

Miamor bit into her inner jaw because she had never hated anyone more than she hated Mecca Diamond, and there were so many emotions pulsing through her body that she could not stop the hot tears from falling down her face.

"See, the bitch does cry," Mecca pointed out to Fabian, who stood baffled behind him. "Now, tell me I'm the best, bitch. Let me hear you say it."

Miamor's body shook with rage as Mecca waited impatiently for her response. Blood poured out of her mouth as she hung in the balance between life and death. She was barely strong enough to hold her head up. As she opened her mouth, she whispered, "Come closer so you can hear me." Barely audible, she waited until Mecca leaned close to her ear. She didn't want him to miss a single word of what she was about to say.

"Say it, bitch. Give up your pride to save your life," Mecca proposed as she breathed in his ear.

"You'll never be the best, Mecca, because I'm the best. You can kill me, but it'll never change the fact that I took everybody you ever loved away from you. You made a mistake when you killed my sister. You take one from me, I take two from you, and the rest of my people are in the wind. They're untouchable. I did that. I made sure of that. If you were the best, you would have done the same. Every day for the rest of your life, you'll think of Miamor, nigga. I promise you," she whispered.

She kissed his cheek, instantly turning his skin cold and running shivers down his spine. It felt like the kiss of death, and Mecca stood to his feet with fire in his eyes. There was nothing he hated more than a slick-talking-ass bitch, but Miamor was like a pit bull; she never let go. Once she put her beam on somebody, nothing could stop her—nothing short of death.

Miamor closed her eyes as she allowed the last tear to fall, then she inhaled deeply before focusing on Mecca, staring him in the eyes. Although he hated her to his core, he knew that they were more alike than either of them had ever cared to admit, and he silently respected her and hated her all in the same moment. They both knew that she had just taken her last breath.

Miamor glared unflinchingly at him and waited for what she knew was to come. It was over, and in that instant, everything went black.

Candles laced the entire basement as the smooth sounds of Bob Marley's "Redemption Song" danced through the airwaves. Marley had a way of speaking to a person's soul and conveying his words on point and full of passion. Ma'tee felt this song more than ever as he closed his eyes and absorbed the powerful lyrics of the legend.

Plush velvet carpet, smells of relaxing lavender incense, and flickering candles all set the mood for what was to be Ma'tee's grand finale. He stared at Breeze, who was lying in the bed dressed in a red lingerie set that he had picked up for her for their special day. He smiled as he looked at Breeze, who was in a dazed-like state, trying to raise her head from the pillow.

It seemed as though a fog had fallen over her. It was as if she were in a hazy dream as she tried to fight the sedation. Ma'tee looked on and smiled at her. "Don't chu try to fight the drug, baby girl. Relax, me lady," he instructed softly as he ran his fingers through her long hair. Ma'tee had heavily drugged her, as he did every night just before he made twisted love to her. In Ma'tee's demented mind, Breeze Diamond was his woman, and he had fallen deeply in love with her over the time she had been in his clutches.

Breeze played the role to the tee as she pretended as if she were off point, but unbeknownst to Ma'tee, Breeze was as clear-headed as she had ever been. Uncharacteristically, Ma'tee had taken his eyes off of Breeze while giving her the drug. Breeze saw an opportunity, and took it by quickly spitting out the pill and pretending as if she had swallowed it. She was just waiting for the right time to make a dash for the stairs that led up to the main floor of Ma'tee's home. Ma'tee was completely naked and ready to lay down with Breeze for the final time, because he had planned for that night to be their last.

As soon as he turns his back, I'm going for it, Breeze thought as nervousness overwhelmed her and her hands began to tremble. Ma'tee turned his back and walked over to the table where the nickel-plated .45 was placed. He was going to shoot Breeze in the head just before he took his own life. In his mind, it was a sure way for them to be together forever. Nevertheless, Breeze had another plan in mind. She was going to break away from Ma'tee—or die trying.

Breeze waited patiently for the right time to make her move and dart for the steps. As soon as Ma'tee's back was totally turned, she took off running as fast as her petite legs could go. She hurriedly skipped two steps at a time, trying to climb to the top.

"Breeze!" Ma'tee yelled as he heard the commotion and saw her take off. He quickly took off after her, remembering that he hadn't locked the door that led to the main floor. "Nooo!" he yelled as he gave chase up the stairs with the gun in his hand.

Breeze sprinted full speed and burst through the door. Her heart began to pound heavily as she was hit by the rays of sunlight shining through the blinds. It had been so long since she had seen sunlight that it was like a punch to the face. Breeze quickly shook off the initial shock and darted out of the basement door, desperately searching for a door to escape the spacious house.

As she frantically ran through the house, Ma'tee was right on her heels. Breeze knocked over lamps and chairs trying to evade his clutches and buy herself more time.

"Please! Let me go!" Breeze pleaded as she approached Ma'tee's front door. But it was to no avail. He had two dead-bolts. She tried to unlock the door quickly, but by that time, Ma'tee had caught up with her and grabbed her from the back. Breeze kicked and screamed, but Ma'tee's strength was too much for her to match. He wrestled her to the floor, and that's when the tears began to pour from Breeze's eyes. She knew that she was about to die. At that very moment, she lost all hope, and her soul no longer belonged to her—it was Ma'tee's.

Ma'tee pointed the gun at Breeze's head and prepared to pull the trigger. "Chu will forever be me lady," he said as he pressed the barrel to Breeze's temple.

Breeze closed her eyes and tried to brace herself for the impact. "God, please have mercy on my soul," she whispered just before the boom. It wasn't a boom from the gun, but the sounds of items falling from Ma'tee's walls and cabinets. The earth began to shake at a magnitude that would be documented in history as one of the worst earthquakes the world had ever seen.

"What the—" Ma'tee tried to stand, but the violent vibrations from the ground knocked him off his feet.

Breeze didn't know what was going on as she looked around, frantically trying to figure out what was the cause of all the rumbling. The ground shook so intensely that Ma'tee's windows shattered and his floor began to crack. The sounds of trees crashing against the earth whistled through the air, and before long, Ma'tee's house began to crumble, as the earth seemed to swallow the house's foundation. Breeze screamed at the top of her lungs. She was in the middle of the pandemonium.

Ma'tee tried to run under his kitchen table for protection, but he never made it. The roof caved in and crushed him, burying him in debris. Breeze witnessed Ma'tee's death just before the roof crushed her also. Breeze was instantly knocked unconscious as the earth crashed down on top of her.

This natural disaster had made an imprint on Haiti's country that would be talked about for years to come.

Carter walked through the cellblock with a folded blanket and thin pillow in his hands. Two guards escorted him to his cell as the sounds of the rowdy inmates echoed through the corridor. Carter walked at his own pace with his head held high. The sound of someone yelling, "The Cartel is in the building!" sounded off, and Carter smirked, knowing that some of his soldiers were on his cellblock. The feds had come in and locked up most of his crew, and some of them were in the same penitentiary Carter was currently at, which meant Carter was still in a position of power.

"Stop right here," the guard said as they approached the last cell on the block.

"Open D-one!" he yelled down the corridor. Moments later, the door slid open, exposing a heavy set Latino man with a salt-and-pepper beard. He looked to be in his mid to late fifties.

"Garza, you have a new celly," the guard said, referring to him having a cellmate.

"You know the rules. My cell is not to be shared!" Garza objected as he sat up from his bunk and placed down the book that he was reading.

"The prison is full and there is no other place he can go. He has to come in here," the guard said as if he were explaining to Garza rather than telling him.

"I don't want a nigger in my cell," Garza said as he gave Carter a dirty look.

Carter nodded and gave Garza a small smirk just to piss him off more.

"It is what it is, Garza. He's your cellmate. Step in," the CO said as he stepped to the side, clearing the way for Carter.

Carter stepped in and placed his things on the top bunk. Moments later, the guard yelled for the cell to be closed and the door slid shut, leaving Garza and Carter alone in the small room.

"Don't get comfortable. You won't be in here for too long," Garza said as he sat back on his bed and focused on his book.

Carter hopped on his bunk and ignored Garza's comment, not wanting to make any enemies so soon. He smirked and shook his head, knowing that Garza didn't realize whom he was talking to, or the power that Carter had. But the truth was that Carter didn't realize the power and connections that Garza possessed.

***

Robyn walked into the crowded courthouse. Her expensive pencil skirt and matching cropped jacket with ruffle top gave her a professional appearance that allowed her to blend in with the lawyers and officials that filled the building. She smiled at the security guard at the entrance as she placed her briefcase on the conveyor belt and then stepped through the metal detector. With her Hermès briefcase in hand and a cardboard tray of Starbucks in the other, she seamlessly bypassed security. Her five-inch heels click clacked across the wooden floor, her step so precise that one would think she was on a runway. She slipped into courtroom A. She peeked at the schedule and noticed that the next trial would not take place for another hour. It was more than enough time to handle her business and disappear.

Just as she suspected, the stenographer was a light-skinned young woman with cute features. The presiding judge had a thing for young black girls. Robyn walked inside and smiled humbly at the girl

"Hi, I'm Vanessa. I'm the new stenographer for Courtroom B. I'm supposed to be training underneath you today," Robyn stated. The lie came off of her lips so smoothly as she put down her things and extended her hand to the girl.

"Oh, no one told me that I was supposed to be training today. Um . . . well . . ." The girl seemed to be put on the spot and completely unprepared for the task at hand.

"I think that they said they were replacing girls because of them being ill prepared," Robyn added slyly as she watched the girl's eyes grow wide in concern.

"Right . . . of course. I remember now . . . the training session today. I'm Melissa," she said as if she had suddenly remembered.

Robyn smiled and grabbed one of the cups of coffee. "Well, Melissa, it's nice to meet you. I can't get through my day without my morning cup of coffee," Robyn said as she extended the cup to the girl. "Consider this as the student bringing the teacher an apple. It's my way of sucking up on the first day."

Melissa accepted the coffee and nodded toward the chamber doors. "You better go introduce yourself to Judge Marrell. That's who you should have purchased coffee for. He's the one to suck up to," Melissa stated playfully.

Robyn winked and replied, "So I've heard." She then made her way to the large wooden door and knocked lightly.

"Come in," she heard the judge say, and she slid inside the plush, prestigious office. The middle-aged white man looked up at her from his desk. "How can I help you?" he asked.

"I'm Vanessa Riley from the District Attorney's office. I'm here to drop off some motions from our office," Robin stated, making up another lie on the spot. She had been doing this for so long that it was nothing for her to switch personas. Lies were more familiar to her than the truth.

"Let's see them, Ms. Riley," he said as he gave her his undivided attention.

Robyn set her briefcase on his desk and unhinged the gold clasps.

"Why haven't I seen you before? I thought I knew everyone from the D.A.'s office," Judge Marrell said.

As Robyn pulled the papers from her briefcase, she replied, "You do know everyone from the D.A.'s office." She smiled and he looked at her curiously. Robyn removed the paperwork from her briefcase and set it in front of the judge.

As the judge looked over the papers, he stated, "What is this? These aren't from the D.A.'s office." He looked up at her in confusion.

"I have a message for you," she stated. She removed a ruler from her briefcase and leaned across the desk. Before he could even protest, she swiped the metal edge across his neck. The normal metal of the ruler had been replaced with a razor blade, and cut through his flesh effortlessly. Blood gushed from his wound as he grasped at his bleeding throat. His eyes widened in fear as he silently pleaded for her to help him.

"Frankie Biggs sends his regards," Robyn stated.

The judge couldn't believe his ears. A man that he had sentenced to life in prison just weeks before had reached out from behind the wall and ordered his execution. For the right price, the Murder Mamas would hit anyone, including a state judge.

As soon as the judge's head hit the wooden desk, Robyn stood up and walked out of his chambers. She bypassed the young girl, Melissa, whose head was face first on her typewriter. The cyanide-laced coffee had done its job to perfection.

Without looking back, Robyn exited the building unnoticed, with a satisfied smirk on her face. She waltzed down the stairs outside the front of the courthouse and slipped into the black Benz that was waiting for her curbside.

Aries pulled away discreetly, and without any words, they got ghost in the wind. Aries felt the engine purr beneath the hood of her Mercedes as she pushed the beautiful car along the California coastline. The wind whipped through Robyn's hair as she pulled off the honey blonde wig that was her disguise.

The mystery that lay behind their designer shades was more deadly than any onlooker could ever imagine. Business was good, as usual. After the tyranny that had taken place in Miami, they had started anew in the City of Angels. There was more money to be made on the West Coast than they had ever encountered before. Leaving bodies in their path, their murder game had soared to new heights.

Still, they couldn't help but feel like a fundamental piece to their puzzle was missing. What had started out as band of five ladies with murder as an agenda had quickly become four, but then four had turned to three, and now after all the bullshit, the last two were standing. Too many mistakes had caused their numbers to dwindle, and not knowing where Miamor was weighed heavily on both of their minds.

The West Coast had been the plan all along. It had all been Miamor's idea. They would take Miami by storm and stack their paper, until Murder was released from prison. That had all been tossed aside when Carter Jones entered the picture. Miamor had forgotten her own rules and gotten so caught up in her emotions that she had broken their cardinal rule: *Money over everything.*

Now Murder was out of prison, Miamor was nowhere to be found, and it was up to them to fill him in on everything that had gone down since the last time he had seen her.

"What are we going to tell him when he asks about her?" Aries asked as they pulled up to the Union Station bus terminal.

"We're going to tell him the truth: Miamor chose a nigga over him and over us," Aries replied uncertainly, knowing that Murder would not receive the news well. When they had contacted him to let him know their whereabouts, they never mentioned that Miamor had not relocated to L.A. They hoped to get him there first and inform him later, because they knew he could help them bring Miamor home and talk some sense into her.

Aries pulled into the parking lot of the station and put the car in park as both she and Robyn peered anxiously toward the door.

"Didn't his bus get here like an hour ago?" Robyn asked.

"He's here. He's watching us. Murder don't move until he's ready to. That's where Miamor got it from," Aries replied confidently as she recalled the many stories that Miamor had shared with her about the man.

Finally, Murder came sauntering out of the station, his pants low, fitted hat worn over his eyes, while his head sat on a swivel neck as he surveyed his surroundings. Even though no pistol dwelled on his hip, his hand was instinctively planted there.

Robyn smirked as she popped the locks for Murder to enter the car. "You're all the way in Cali. Who you looking for?"

Her tone was playful, but his was not when he replied, "I've popped niggas in Cali." With that, he ducked low in his seat and pulled down his hat as Aries put the car in drive.

"Where's Miamor?" he asked immediately. She was whom he had made the trip to see. After years of lockup, their reunion was inevitable.

"We have something to tell you." Robyn turned around so that she was facing Murder. "In the letter we sent you, we didn't tell you everything."

"Where's Miamor?" Murder asked again, almost impatiently.

Aries was silent as she drove. She didn't want to be the bearer of bad news. The hairs on the back of her neck stood up as Robyn spoke up.

"She's not here. She decided to stay in Miami. She's fucking with the same niggas that murdered Anisa," Robyn stated.

Murder's temperature went through the roof as his jaw tightened and his brown eyes turned black. "My li'l mama wouldn't do that," Murder replied assuredly as he stretched out across the backseat of the car.

"It's not exactly how Robyn is making it sound," Aries cut in. "When we went to Miami, we accepted a contract to hit a group called The Cartel. Anisa was murdered, and after that, everything spun out of control. Miamor met this nigga named

Carter. She fell in love with him, but did not know that he was affiliated with The Cartel."

"Affiliated how?" Murder asked. His words were calm, but the blaze behind his stare revealed his true emotions.

"He's the brother of the nigga that killed Anisa," Robyn finished. "When we left, she stayed behind. She's not the same, Murder. That nigga Carter got her all fucked up in the head, and we need your help to get her back."

Murder was livid as he processed everything the Murder Mamas had told him. He had been gone for too long. He was out of touch with the streets, and even worse, out of touch with Miamor. Although he had never expected her to wait for him, hearing that she was so loyal to another man sparked a flame inside of him that he tried to snuff out long ago. He was ready to go retrieve Miamor, and anybody who stood between them could get it.

They rode in silence, until they reached the condo that Robyn and Aries shared. As they walked up their walkway, they immediately noticed that things were not as they left them. The curtains in the living room window had been shifted slightly, and the piece of clear tape that they had put at the top of their front door had been ripped in half, indicating that someone had come in or out of the condo.

Aries put her finger to her lips and pulled out her 9 mm pistol as she stepped into the condo first. Their place was untouched; nothing was out of place, but they knew that someone had crossed their threshold. They filtered through the place, going in separate directions, until every room had been checked.

"There's nobody here," Murder stated.

"But somebody's been here," Robyn stated as she finally noticed the medium- sized packing box that sat in the middle of their kitchen island. She picked it up, and Aries gasped as she noticed the blood-stained bottom.

"Robyn," she said as she pointed at the red color.

Murder walked over to her and removed the box from her hands.

He opened the box, and when he noticed what was inside, his stomach folded, causing him to bend over as if someone had punched him in the gut.

"What is it?" Aries asked in a panic as she watched Murder's reaction.

Tears filled Robyn's eyes as she shook her head back and forth in disbelief. She ran over to the kitchen sink as the contents of her stomach erupted from her mouth.

"What the fuck is it?" Aries asked again as she stormed over to the box, but Murder stopped her in her tracks as he wrapped one hand around her throat.

"Why did you leave her there?" he asked. "You should have never left her in Miami!" he stated, his eyes ablaze with anger.

The mixture of devastation and rage that twisted his features told Aries all that she needed to know. She violently slapped his hand away from her neck and rushed over to the box. Her heart felt as if it shattered into tiny pieces when she saw the severed hand that lay inside. The cursive *Murder Mama* on the wrist revealed her identity. It was Miamor. They knew that only one person could be this ruthless.

"She's dead," Aries whispered in disbelief.

Robyn stood from the sink and walked over to Aries as they wrapped their arms around each other. "We shouldn't have left her," Aries whispered regretfully.

There was an address written on the inside of Miamor's hand. It was a sign of respect that only someone in their profession would understand. It was Mecca's way of letting them know where they could find her body.

Without turning around, Murder stated, "I want to know everything you know about The Cartel." No more words needed to be spoken. They all knew what had to be done. It was time to go back to Miami.

Welcome to

THE CARTEL 3

Chapter Two

"Please, God, let somebody come for me."
—*Breeze*

Every inch of Breeze's body ached unbearably as the weight of Ma'tee's home rested on top of her. "Help me!" she screamed, her voice raspy and sore from strain. For two days, she had been trapped beneath the rubble. She was trapped next to Ma'tee's decaying body, and the smell was slowly driving her insane. His dead eyes haunted her as they stared in her direction. She could still hear his voice in her head, terrorizing her, telling her that she would never escape, and she felt nothing but utter hopelessness, because she knew that no one even knew where to begin looking for her.

Breeze's body wanted to give out on her. Without food she was weak, but she knew that she could not give into death. She had to make it out of this alive. She had come too far to die now. Ma'tee could no longer hold her captive.

All I have to do is hold on. Someone will come, she thought. *They have to.* She sucked on the wet dirt beneath her to provide herself with some type of water. It was all that her body was surviving on, but she knew that it would not be enough for her to make it much longer. Being trapped beneath the steel and concrete was like being buried alive.

Physically, she knew that she was injured, but she blocked out the pain as she tried to keep her mind strong. She knew that once her will disappeared she would die, so she tried her best to remain calm. Her father had always told her that panic sent logic right out the window, and she would need to think clearly in order to survive.

The excruciating heat made her feel as if she were roasting in a cement oven. The blocks resting on top of her baked beneath the sun all day, burning her so badly that it felt as if a hot iron were being placed to her skin.

She was grateful when the sun began to set, but the night brought on a completely different set of problems for Breeze. The sounds of the jungle terrified her, as the wildlife was attracted to the scent of Ma'tee's corpse. She wished that she could cover her ears, but her hands were smashed beneath the rock, and the only thing she could do was close her eyes.

Zyir's face popped into her mind as she tuned out the sounds of the night. He had always been her voice of reason when she needed him, and as she visualized him in her mind, she realized that she couldn't quite remember all of the details of his face. Too much time had passed, and she no longer held his exact features to memory. It was then that she grew more determined than ever to make it home. *Please, God, let somebody come for me,* she prayed.

She had very little faith that her prayers would be answered. Speaking to God had not saved her from Ma'tee's torture, so she was skeptical that He would spare her from this. She was tired of the hardship that had become her life, and a part of her wished that she had been the one to die when the earthquake first hit. It seemed that Ma'tee had been granted the easy way out, while she was left to suffer.

She could feel herself dying slowly. With every minute that passed, her heartbeat slowed down. It was only a matter of time before it gave out. Breeze suffered through the sounds of the night with her eyes closed, but sleep never came. Her nerves were too on edge for her to rest. The ground had not stopped shaking beneath her. Every few hours, another aftershock set off more destruction, shifting the house on top of her and causing her even more pain. The threat of it falling in on her completely was a constant threat. Any second she could be crushed to death, and the impending circumstance caused her body to tremble.

She began to talk to herself just to stay lucid, singing songs that she remembered to stop herself from giving in to the pain. Everything in her just wanted to let the earth swallow her. Exhaustion and fatigue caused her eyelids to become heavy.

Just as the daylight came creeping back across the horizon, she heard the sound of human voices. She strained to listen, thinking that her mind was playing an evil trick on her.

"Hello? Is anyone out there?" she called out at the top of her lungs. When she didn't hear a response, her heart dropped in disappointment, but the footsteps around her grew increasingly more audible. Straining her ears, she finally confirmed the voices. She could not make out what they were saying, but it didn't matter; she could not let them pass her by.

"Help! Help me!" she yelled desperately as she pushed against the rock, steel, and slate that imprisoned her. She screamed so loudly that her lungs hurt and she choked on the dust in the air, but she did not stop until she got the attention of the men. After locating her voice underneath the ominous pile, they rushed to her aid.

"Get me out! Get me out!" she cried frantically. "Please hurry!" She panicked as she felt the men lifting the concrete from her body. The closer they got to rescuing her, the more Breeze hyperventilated. Relief washed over her as she wept loudly. She had never been so glad to hear another human voice.

The men worked diligently to dig Breeze out as they spoke in a native Haitian dialect that she could not understand. They had no machines or forklifts, only their bare hands and the strength that God had given them, but that did not stop them from helping Breeze. Although a language barrier stopped them from communicating, they knew what the look in her eyes meant. They could see her pleading with them to get her out.

The more weight that was lifted off of Breeze, the more pain she felt. Her legs were completely useless. The blood flow had been cut off from them, and her light skin had turned a sickening blue.

Once they could maneuver her out, one of the men picked her up, while the others began to dig out Ma'tee.

"No!" she yelled. The men looked at her in confusion, but none of them stopped digging. They refused to leave a man behind. When they finally removed Ma'tee from the rubble, they realized that he was already dead. They debated whether they should carry his body down the mountain, but there was no point in wasting their energy on him. Even if they did take his body to the town, it would just lie out in the streets. No one who died in this tragedy would receive a proper burial, so they figured it best to just let him be.

Breeze let her head rest against the chest of one of the rescuers as they began their descent down the mountain. Not once did she look back. She was eager for help, and expected to be rescued as soon as they finished their descent down the mountain. She was unprepared for the chaos that awaited her in the city of Port-au-Prince. Everything had been destroyed, and there were too many people to help and not enough relief to make a difference.

The men dropped Breeze off at a safety site that had been set up, and went on their way. It was a free for all; everyone was out for self, and the lack of organization gave her no one to turn to. She was left to fend for herself.

The safety site looked more like a demolition site to Breeze. Makeshift tents had been made out of sheets and spare fabric to cover some of the injured people being treated by the doctors. The chaos was overwhelming as Breeze surveyed the aftermath of the quake. Trapped atop the mountain with Ma'tee, she had no idea how big the earthquake really was.

The magnitude of its destruction was unimaginable. Everyone was displaced, everyone was injured, everyone needed help. This natural disaster had destroyed an entire nation of people, so much so that even the organizations that had come to help did not know where to start.

Breeze had been one of the lucky ones. She had made it out of the rubble. She was cut badly, bruised beyond belief, and starving for nutrition, but she was alive, and as she looked around sadly at all of the dead bodies, she realized how grateful she was.

When the circulation finally came back to her legs, she walked aimlessly, trying not to stare at the lost children who walked the streets, many in search of parents they would never find. Their cries made her cringe because she knew exactly how it felt to be ripped from those you love.

American camera crews recorded the horrendous tragedy, and even CNN's Anderson Cooper reported live in an attempt to display what was happening to the world. Haiti had been impoverished for years, but the earthquake had put the international spotlight on the black nation.

Breeze was dumbfounded because although America was reporting on the situation, she never saw one reporter put down their microphones to assist or offer help. When the little red lights of their camera came on and the crew was filming, they were engaged and sympathetic, but when it came down to actually contributing to humanity, they all recoiled selfishly. As soon as the cameras stopped rolling, their concern for the earthquake victims dwindled, proving to Breeze that it was all for show. There were people dying around them, and all they cared about was the story.

She was in desperate need of medical attention, sustaining not only injuries from the quake, but also injuries from being raped by Ma'tee. She was physically, psychologically, and emotionally troubled, but as she looked around her, she realized that that was not only her story, but the story of so many others as well.

There was no food, no water, no relief whatsoever, and Haitian citizens were beginning to get restless. Breeze watched as gangs of individuals looted whatever places were still standing in attempts to find supplies and food. The scarcity of resources was making everyone desperate, and as Breeze noticed a fruit truck being looted, she could not stop herself from following suit. The hunger pangs shooting through her stomach justified her actions as she ran over to the truck and pushed her way to the front to grab her share. After filling her hands with four large oranges, she attempted to run, but was stopped by a woman who was fighting to snatch the fruit from Breeze.

"No," Breeze protested as she pushed the woman off of her violently. She ran away from the scene and found an empty cot near the safety site. She collapsed as she tore open the fruit and sucked the juices from the inside. She resembled an animal as she ate ravenously, keeping her eyes up as she guarded the only meal she had received in days.

Her heart tore in half when she saw a little girl eyeing her desperately. Breeze knew that her soul had disappeared when she shouted, "What the hell are you looking at? I don't have anything for you!"

It was then that she realized that Ma'tee really had turned her soul black. Before landing in his company, she had been selfless and giving. Even amongst the worst of predicaments Breeze had always maintained a good heart.

Guilt plagued her as she looked down at the three other pieces of fruit she had stolen. "Here," she said to the small child as she held out an orange for the girl. The little girl's eyes lit up as she thankfully took the fruit.

They sat eating the meager meal together as if it would be their last. Breeze did not know what her next move would be. Waiting would be like torture, but she had no other choice. She didn't know if she was waiting to live or waiting to die; she only hoped that a resolution would eventually come.

Chapter Three

"The connect ain't fucking with us because we got that federal eye in the sky on us."
–Zyir

Mecca sat back in the large meeting room of the Diamond family mansion. Pretty soon it would belong to someone else. Mecca had put the beautiful property up for sale. It was too hot, and now it was time to rebuild the Diamond legacy somewhere else. Everything had been cleared out except for this one room.

He closed his eyes as his mind drifted back to the days when his father used to hold court for his head lieutenants in that very space. It seemed that his father had run things so smoothly. The Cartel of today was a far cry from the organized crime family his father had started. Now everything around them was chaos, and with Young Carter in jail, Mecca was unsure if he could fill the shoes of the leader and effectively run The Cartel.

It was no longer a family operation. Only one Diamond was left standing, and although Carter was his half-brother, it wasn't the same. They had suffered too many casualties, and loyalty was a rarity nowadays. His father had ruled with love, whereas now Carter, Mecca, and Zyir were holding down their spot in the streets with fear.

With the spotlight of the feds shining on them, nobody

wanted to deal to closely with The Cartel. The streets were talking, and word was out that Carter just might lose his case. Niggas from the bottom to the top were shook, including their coke supplier.

The sound of the foyer door opening snapped him out of his reverie, and he stood to welcome Zyir.

"What's good, fam?" Zyir greeted as he embraced Mecca briefly.

"You tell me. How's that paper looking?" Mecca asked.

As The Cartel's most trusted lieutenant, Zyir's ear was glued to the street. There was nothing that got by him. Mecca had been forced to lay low because of his beef with Emilio Estes, so it was up to Zyir to ensure that their presence remained known in the streets.

"Shit is slow. Carter's case got everybody running scared. The connect ain't fucking with us because we got that federal eye in the sky on us, nah mean?"

"What about the niggas that owe us money?" Mecca asked irritably. It seemed as if everything they had built was now on the downfall.

"Oh, I got that cake . . . believe that. Ain't nobody skipping out on the bill, but nobody's re-upping. It's like niggas is cutting ties. Nobody wants to be associated with a sinking ship. Niggas only loyal when the getting is good. I mean, we still got a few men who standing tall, but I ain't gon' lie. Shit ain't sweet," Zyir informed. "With everything seized, that shoebox money running real low. Carter's lawyer expecting another payment today, and even my stash is hurting."

Mecca knew that things would get tight for everybody with Carter locked up. The government had frozen all of their legitimate accounts; even Diamond Realty profits could not be touched until a resolution to Carter's case was reached. Everyone, including Mecca, was living temporarily off of whatever money had flown under the radar; but random money that had been stashed in safes wasn't enough for men who spent it as if it grew on trees. Between the two of them, they had a little over a million dollars, but with Carter's case eating into their finances and a paranoid cocaine connection, that large sum of petty cash was dwindling by the day.

"What time do you have to meet the lawyers?" Mecca asked.

"In about an hour. After that, I plan on checking in with Carter. I need to let him know what's going on, and he's been asking me to check for his chick, Miamor," Zyir replied.

"Tell him to stop looking," Mecca stated coldly.

"What?" Zyir questioned. "You know he ain't gonna stop looking for her. That's his bitch."

Mecca removed the scowl from his face and replied, "I heard she left town, so tell him to stop worrying about a bitch. We gotta keep his mind right so he can beat this case."

Overwhelmed and worried about the state of his family's empire, Mecca sighed. "I'll drop that payment off to the lawyer. You holla at Carter. Let him know what's been going on. See what he want us to do to stay afloat."

As Mecca watched Zyir leave, he collapsed back into his father's chair. The throne that he had sat on for many years seemed too big for Mecca, the responsibilities of heading The Cartel too daunting for a hothead like Mecca. Mecca was built to be in the game. He was a goon, a killer, and his natural born hustle was innate, but being the leader had never been his forte. That role had better suited his twin brother, Money.

The thought of Monroe brought tears to his eyes. He had hardened himself to insanity after he had murdered his brother, but the extreme guilt that still plagued him over his actions always broke him down. On the rare moments when he was alone and had time to reflect, he remembered that fateful night, and he mourned the lost of his other half. Monroe was his only weakness—and his murder was a secret that Mecca would take to his grave.

Zyir sat across from Carter, six inches of glass separating them from one another, and Zyir felt a sense of despair on behalf of his mentor. Carter was his brother, and in a way, the only father figure that Zyir had ever had. It pained Zyir to see him confined, his usual designer threads replaced by an orange jumpsuit.

Carter had taught Zyir everything he knew about the game. Carter had groomed him for this exact moment because he understood that the game did not last forever, and once he met his downfall, he was confident that Zyir would be able to take his place.

"How you holding up?" Zyir asked as he gripped the telephone, obviously uncomfortable within the confines of the federal penitentiary. There was something about being behind those walls that terrified Zyir, despite the fact that his own freedom wasn't at risk.

"Wipe that sad look off your face, li'l nigga. You look like you're standing over my casket or something," Carter joked charismatically while smirking.

Zyir loosened up a little and chuckled a bit before replying, "Just don't feel right, nah mean? Looking at you through this glass. We working on that as we speak. Got your legal peoples working around the clock on your case."

Carter respected Zyir for his loyalty and support. Carter wasn't an optimist, however. He was a realist, and he wanted to prepare his little nigga for his potential conviction.

"Zy . . . Carter cleared his throat and rubbed his growing goatee as he stared intently at his protégé. You know there's a possibility that this could all end badly for me.

Zyir shook his head in denial and replied, "Nah, fam. Shit is going to work itself out. Before you know it, you'll be home."

Carter nodded his head and didn't press the issue further. He just wanted to put it out there. He knew Zyir like the back of his hand. He had planted the seed in Zyir's head, and knew that Zyir would make the necessary plans just in case.

"Why hasn't Miamor been to see me? I can't reach her by phone. Have you heard from her?" Carter inquired.

Zyir shook his head. He hated to be the one to tell him the news, but thought he deserved to know. "Mecca heard she skipped town right after your arrest," Zyir stated.

Carter frowned and replied, "Skipped town?" The news was disturbing to hear. Nothing about it resonated as true in his heart. His case had nothing to do with her, and he knew that the only time a bitch was leaving town was if she was running away with a bag full of money. Miamor never had access to his paper, and he had never involved her in his illegal dealings, so she had no reason to run. It didn't make sense to him, but he knew that he was in no position to worry about her whereabouts. If and when he got out of prison, he would handle the situation; until then, he stored the information in his mental Rolodex.

After Zyir informed him of the state of The Cartel, their visit was cut short. He had a lot to think about. He had played the game for many years, and now it seemed that it had finally caught up to him. His judgment day had arrived.

Mecca emerged from the family mansion cautiously as he looked around him in paranoia. He knew that his grandfather, Emilio Estes, would not stop until his head was on a platter, and that his power was far reaching. Mecca had no idea who Estes was going to send at him, so he watched his back wherever he went. He slid into his Lamborghini and left rubber in his path as he sped off toward the lawyer's office.

Alton Beckham was a defense attorney who had been on retainer from the very beginning. A friend to his father, Mecca knew that Beckham was Young Carter's best chance of getting off. His unscrupulous morals and greed for money were the main reasons why he was so beneficial to his clients.

Mecca walked into his office, where Beckham's receptionist greeted him. She stood to greet Mecca.

"Hello, Mr. Diamond. If you'll have a seat, Mr. Beckham has another client in his office, but—"

Before she could even finish her sentence, Mecca bypassed the secretary as if she were invisible and walked directly into Beckham's office.

"I'm sorry, Mr. Beckham," the secretary stated as she rushed inside behind Mecca. "I told him he had to wait."

"I don't wait," Mecca stated simply as he took a seat next to the client that was already sitting, with no regard for the meeting that he was interrupting.

Beckham stood up from behind his desk. "It's okay, Tracy. Mr. Diamond is always welcome." He then turned to his client and extended his hand. "I apologize, but I'm going to have to cut our meeting short. You can reschedule out front." Knowing exactly who Mecca Diamond was, the other client didn't protest before walking out of the room.

Once the office was clear, Beckham got down to business. He loosened his tie and sat back in his plush leather chair as he reached underneath his desk, pulling out a bottle of cognac. He poured two glasses and then held one out to Mecca.

Mecca smirked at the Jewish lawyer before him. "Every time I accept a drink from you, bad news follows." Mecca was only half joking. He knew that Beckham was a beast in the courtroom, but he was a snake outside of it. He offered his expertise, but it came at a hefty price.

"Carter's case requires more time than I previously anticipated. The federal prosecutor really has a hard-on for your brother. He's doing everything he can in order to send Carter away. They don't just want a conviction; they want a life sentence, and they want to make an example out of The Cartel. In order for me to prepare the best defense, I'm going to have to go up on my price."

"Don't beat around the bush, Beckham. The bottom line is money. How much do you want?" Mecca asked. "I brought a payment here for you today." Mecca placed a money-filled manila envelope in front of the lawyer. "Fifty thousand dollars."

Trusting his long working relationship with the Diamond family, Beckham did not feel the need to count it. He put it in his desk drawer and replied, "That's a start."

"What price will finish it?" Mecca questioned.

"Double," Beckham responded.

Mecca did not have a problem paying the fee. It was worth Carter's freedom, but he wanted to make it clear that if he was going to spare no expense, then Carter's freedom better be guaranteed.

"You know, with that type of paper, you'll have new responsibilities. I will personally expect more from you. You accepting that type of money tells me that my brother will walk. Things could turn out real bad for you if you don't live up to these expectations. You understand?" Mecca asked boldly.

Beckham was well aware of who he was dealing with, and he knew that by charging The Cartel double for their leader's defense, he was playing with his own life. If he lost, the consequences would be devastating for him, but greed outweighed his reason. "I understand," he replied as he extended his hand.

Once Mecca accepted it, the new deal was done. Getting Carter out of prison would not be cheap, but it was worth it, because only Carter had the foresight it took to get The Cartel out of its slump. He could re-establish their cocaine connection. Once Carter was out, everyone would eat again, and the balance of power would be restored.

Mecca emerged from the attorney's office and removed his car keys from his back pocket. When he was halfway across the street, he hit the remote starter on his keychain.

BOOM!

Glass and metal flew everywhere as Mecca's car exploded, knocking him from his feet and sending him flying backward onto the pavement.

"Oh shit!" he yelled out in panicked alarm as he scrambled to his feet and backpedaled away from the blaze. He looked around in bewilderment as flames engulfed his five-figure car and a crowd began to draw around him. "Fuck!" he yelled as he put his hands on the side of his head. He knew that only one person would have the balls to come after him—Emilio Estes—and as he looked on in pure rage, he knew that this was far from being over. His grandfather would not stop until he put Mecca in a grave—right next to his twin brother.

Leena sat in the opulence of the oceanside villa that was now her home. She could not believe that her life had come to this point. She had played a dangerous game by falling in love with two brothers, and the end result had proven deadly. She could still feel the ache where Mecca's bullet had penetrated her, but it didn't hurt nearly as much as the fact that she had sparked a beef between two brothers.

She had created a divide between two men who should have been inseparable . . . impenetrable . . . invincible, but because of her, everything had been torn apart.

She smiled as she looked at her child, Monroe's only son, as he sat playing quietly on the floor beneath her feet. The only living seed of the late Monroe Diamond sat so innocently, so unaware of his status. He was the heir to so much power and money. Her son was a Diamond, and it was that fact that kept her safe. It kept her alive. It had made her untouchable.

She had been whisked away from the hospital to this world of luxury. She had been there for over a year, and now she sat eating nervously, silently, across from Emilio Estes, the man who had made it all possible. Her child had given her access to the throne, a throne so much bigger than she had ever been appointed.

The Dominican born Estes was more powerful than anyone she had ever met, including the Diamond brothers. He was their grandfather, and now he was her provider.

As she picked at the chef-prepared meal before her, she kept her eyes on her plate. She could feel the power emanating from him all the way across the table. He intimidated her; there was a mysterious nature to him. He was a man of few words, and during the time that they had spent together, he asked more questions than he ever answered. He observed her, and although she felt sheltered around him, she still feared him.

What does he want from me? Why am I really here? she asked herself.

He insisted that she stay with him, but in spite of the time that she had been a guest in his house, she still did not know him. Estes spared her nothing and lavishly showered her with gifts. She was his unspoken possession, one that was well kept and polished. He had expressed his interests in her by giving her material things and security. He ensured that her every need was attended to, but for Leena, love was elusive. She knew that she could never give Estes what he sought.

He kept her around as the lady on his arm, but the only reason she allowed him to was because she had no other choice. How could she turn down the man who had taken her in after she had been shot? He had nursed her back to health and saw her through her entire pregnancy. He had treated her well, and because of this, she felt indebted to him.

"What is it that you want from me?" she asked as she finally mustered the courage to look up at him across the long dining room table.

He was reading the daily newspaper while sipping coffee, and he took his time before he acknowledged her question. Her stomach was in knots as she watched him. He always moved in his own time, and his silence caused her heart to gallop in anxiety.

"I just want you to care for my great-grandson. That's all I require of you," he replied without looking up from his newspaper.

"That's my responsibility as a mother. I understand that you want your great-grandson to be here with you, but why am I here?" she asked.

"I hoped that you would allow me to share in his life with you. I told you that my lineage would always be taken care of. You are the mother to my grandson's first born. Monroe would have taken very good care of you if he could have. In his absence, I plan to ensure that you want for nothing; that my great-grandson wants for nothing. I have become very fond of you since you have been here. I know that you are reluctant to return my affections, but you are young, and your heart is still broken from losing Monroe. In time, I hope that your heart will warm to me."

Leena nodded, but could not find the words to respond. Her emotions were so mixed when it came to her situation. She was more appreciative than anything. He was so kind and so generous, but she could not help but to walk around on eggshells.

To be in the presence of a man so great would take some getting used to, but Estes had already established that he wanted her around, and she was silently relieved to have his support. In honesty, she was still afraid of Mecca. She knew that he had cared deeply for her, and her betrayal had pushed him over the edge. He did not know that she had survived, and she was afraid that if he ever found out, he would finish what he started. By choosing to be with Estes, she knew that Mecca couldn't touch her, and that alone was reason enough for her to stay, despite the fact that her heart was not fully invested.

Chapter Four

"It doesn't feel as good as the first time."
—*Breeze*

The chaos around her was overwhelming as the devastation of the earthquake displayed itself all around her. Escaping Ma'tee's imprisonment should have brought some type of relief, but being free was overshadowed by the catastrophe that had occurred. Her bruised and cut up body was nothing compared to the dead bodies that littered the streets, decomposing before her terrified eyes. The overwhelming heat mixed with the smell of death in the air caused her insides to erupt. She had thrown up so many times that she had lost count, and with no clean drinking water in sight, she had nothing to replace the energy that was leaving her body. She could barely breathe because the stench was so horrifying. She had never yearned for home more than she did at that moment.

Her heart raced every second because she did not know what to expect next. The unstable ground beneath her threatened to crack every time the earth shook. How had she come to be so far away from the safety of the Diamond mansion? Her life had been a living hell, and Mother Earth was taking no prisoners as it destroyed everything in its path. The people of Haiti had just had everything stripped from them, and Breeze was amongst them. The little bit of hope that she had left had been buried underneath the rubble. She was going to die in Haiti. What Ma'tee did not finish, Mother Earth surely would.

As Breeze lay on the blood-stained cot out in the open sun, it felt as if she were baking alive. Her light skin had burnt badly, causing her open wounds to crust over with infection. It was so hot that the vision before her eyes was hazy, as if steam was rising from the cracks in the ground. Circumstances had never been so dire. Breeze's survival was out of her hands, and as the bodies continued to drop like flies around her, she silently feared that she would be next.

Breeze could barely lift her head as she watched those around her. She noticed a white woman going around with water-filled canteens. Too weak to even call out, she silently prayed for the woman to come her way. She noticed how the woman picked some of the younger ladies to follow her as she made her way through the thick crowd. It was as if the woman was looking for someone in particular.

When the woman finally crossed Breeze's path, she reached out her arm and grabbed the woman's leg in desperation. The woman turned to Breeze and stared down at her in sympathy.

"Please. I need water," Breeze whispered, her eyes pleading.

"Of course," the woman replied as she knelt beside Breeze. She motioned for the young women who followed her to halt, and then she lifted the canteen to Breeze's lips.

Breeze greedily gulped the water, the coolness of the liquid soothing her dry insides. She closed her eyes. Nothing had ever been so satisfying.

The woman could not see Breeze's face through all of the dirt and ash that covered it. She smiled slightly as she wiped the dirt from Breeze's ashen features, trying to show her a friendly face amongst the debris and turmoil.

"I'm Ms. Beth," the woman stated. "What is your name?" she asked.

"Breeze," she responded as she continued to drink the water, hydrating her soul as much as her body.

"Breeze, where is your family?" Ms. Beth asked.

The thought of her loved ones brought tears of pain to her eyes. She had not seen them in so long. Her heart broke to pieces as she began to sob. "I don't know. I'm not even supposed to be here," she cried.

"Come on, sweetheart. I can take you somewhere safe," Ms. Beth stated as she helped Breeze to her feet. Feeling a sense of trust for the first time since she had been taken away from her family, Breeze stood on her shaky limbs and joined the small group of young women as they walked behind Ms. Beth.

"Where is she taking us?" Breeze asked one of the girls who walked beside her.

"She came through here yesterday and helped a lot of people. She gave them water and food, then she took them somewhere safe. I think she works for a charity in the States. I hope that she is taking us there. I've always wanted to go there," the young Haitian girl said whimsically.

"She's taking us to the Unites States?" Breeze repeated. Her heart fluttered as visions of home flooded her mind.

The girl nodded her head, and it was all the confirmation that Breeze needed to continue to follow Ms. Beth as if she were the shepherd leading her sheep. Breeze looked back at what was left of the city of Port-au-Prince, and she was just grateful that an opportunity to get out had arisen. She had thought that she would be forever lost in the buried city, but Ms. Beth had just come to her rescue.

They walked for miles before Breeze finally saw the boat. It looked like a large military ship. The massive piece of steel that sat in the water sent shivers down her spine, and as Breeze looked on at the group of girls she stood amongst, she recognized the same glimmer of hope in everyone's eyes. All they wanted to do was get to a better place, to feel safe. Even though the boat was daunting, it was their only way out, and none of them was going to deny it.

Breeze's eyes fell upon the side of the medium-sized vessel. The word MURDERVILLE had been graffiti-painted on the ship's starboard side.

Breeze wanted to call her family so badly to let them know that she was alive and that she was safe. They were the first people she wanted to see when she finally made it to the States.

There were about fifty other girls all around her who were just as eager as Breeze, but all of their fear originated from the quake. Breeze's torture had included so much more. The rape, the kidnapping, the degradation from Ma'tee was a precursor to this natural disaster, and if she did not speak to her family soon, she was sure that her sanity would crack. Overwhelmed and anxious, she pushed through the crowd to get to Ms. Beth.

"Ms. Beth!" Breeze called out to get her attention amongst the many young women. As Ms. Beth tried to organize the crowd, Breeze followed behind her. "Ms. Beth, do you have a cell phone that I can use? I haven't talked to my family in so long. I just want to let them know that I'm coming home. They don't even know I'm alive."

Ms. Beth was too busy to stop her stride, but Breeze followed behind her as she watched everyone begin to form a line.

"I'm sorry, Breeze. I don't have a phone that is available for you right now. There's no service on this side of the island. As soon as we reach the States, I will get you to a phone so that you can call your family," Ms. Beth stated. She could see the disappointment in Breeze's eyes, so she put one hand on her shoulder and added, "Don't worry. Everything will be fine now. You will be back with them before you know it."

Breeze nodded.

"Now, go ahead and get in line so that you can get your vaccination. We can't have you bringing any diseases back to the U.S. with you," Ms. Beth said reassuringly.

Breeze got into the line, and when it was her turn to receive the medicine, Ms. Beth tied a thick rubber band around her arm, causing a huge vein to emerge. Ms. Beth smiled at Breeze and said, "I promise all of your pain will go away, Breeze."

"I hope so," Breeze answered back through tear-filled eyes. Ms. Beth stuck the needle in Breeze's arm and injected it slowly. As the drug entered her system, a warm, euphoric feeling traveled up her arm and spread throughout her entire body.

"You'll be tired for a while, but this will keep you from getting sick. A disaster this big brings about a lot of infection," Ms. Beth stated. "There will be a cot for you to rest on once you're on board."

Breeze nodded, but really did not pay attention to anything that Ms. Beth said. The euphoric feeling that took over her body made all of her worries, all of her pain, and all of the horrible memories of Ma'tee's abuse go away instantly. Her eyelids felt so heavy that she could barely keep them from closing, and her mouth fell open slightly in satisfaction. Every spot on her body tingled, and her clitoris hardened as the drug surged through her veins. Breeze felt so good that she came to an orgasm where she stood, causing the place between her legs to become wet with her own juices. She obediently fell in line as she followed the rest of the girls onto the boat.

Breeze awoke to the prick of another needle being put into her arm. This time, it wasn't by Ms. Beth, but one of the men she had seen when she boarded the boat back in Haiti. As she looked around, she noticed that the other girls were being injected as well. She wanted to ask what they were giving her, but as quickly as the thought of protest popped into her mind, the drug took its effect and erased any objection that she had. A stupid grin spread across her face as her neck muscles weakened slightly, causing her head to dip onto her chest. Nothing had ever felt better, and she welcomed the sensations that traveled through her.

She had no idea that Ms. Beth and her team were forcing heroin into her system. All she knew was that the medicine made her feel good. It made everything feel like bliss, and numbed her emotions to the point where she forgot about all that had happened. She was almost drunk with ecstasy as her body began to warm. It did not feel as good as the first dose, and as the man stood to move to the next girl, Breeze grabbed his arm.

"Can you give me a little more? It doesn't feel as good as the first time," she whispered.

The man chuckled and shook his head. "It never does, sweetheart," he replied before moving on to his next victim.

Ms. Beth was in the business of human trafficking, and went from impoverished island to impoverished island in the Caribbean to lure young women and children with the hopes of a better life. The children that she abducted were usually trafficked into modern day slavery, but the young women were like budding flowers and were picked for the sex trade.

When she stumbled across Breeze, she knew that she had hit the jackpot. Her American clients would go crazy over the young beauty, and she would make a big profit off of her because of her fair skin tone.

The heroin made it easier to take advantage of her victims. The drug kept them under control and dependent. Breeze had just been introduced to the world of addiction, and she would always chase the potency of the first high that she had been given. Her ignorance would only last for so long, and by the time she realized that she was hooked, it would be too late for her to stop. Even though she was on her way back to the United States, she was now more far away from home than she had ever been. Now she was lost in a boy that was so strong that once he got a hold of you, he rarely ever let go.

After two days of traveling underneath the deck of the ship, Breeze was relieved when the boat finally docked. Breeze rushed up the stairs. The door leading to the main deck was always locked. The girls traveling below were not allowed on the main deck, and as they traveled, they had confined below, anxiously awaiting their arrival. For many of them, it was the start of a new life. For Breeze, it would be a return to her old one. Breeze beat the door with her fists as she anticipated the reunion she would have with her family.

The door opened, and Breeze rushed out only to be stopped by one of Ms. Beth's workers.

"What are you doing? Let me go. I just want to see where we are," Breeze shouted as she struggled against the man.

It wasn't until she felt the hard sting of his hand that her instincts told her something was horribly wrong. Now that her high had worn off, she was able to process the situation in a new light. She did not know what was going on, but now that they were back in the U.S., she wanted off of that boat. "Where's Ms. Beth? I need to speak to her!" she yelled persistently as she was pushed back beneath the deck. "She said I could make a call."

At that moment, the metal door opened and Ms. Beth walked down with five men following behind her.

"Ms. Beth!" Breeze shouted as she pushed past the man apprehending her. "Where are we? I felt the boat dock. You said I could call my family," she reminded desperately, but as Breeze spoke, she noticed that the disposition of the friendly woman she had met in Haiti had changed. Her eyes were cold and revealed sinister intentions as she stared unflinchingly back at Breeze.

Her father always told her she could see the character of a person by looking in their eyes, and as Breeze studied Ms. Beth, she finally saw the devil that dwelled inside of her. Her brow furrowed in confusion.

"You said you would help me get home!" Breeze shouted as she watched Ms. Beth's staff filter through the room and begin to blast heroin into the other girls' arms.

Breeze backed away from Ms. Beth as she looked down at her own arms. Non-stop needles had been put into her veins for the past forty-eight hours, and foolishly, Breeze had allowed them to do it.

"What have you been giving me?" she screamed hysterically. "Why are you doing this?" Breeze demanded.

"Restrain her," Ms. Beth said calmly to one of her workers.

"You bitch!" Breeze yelled as she charged Ms. Beth. She smacked fire from Ms. Beth before she was finally subdued, and she screamed like a mad woman as she watched the woman who she thought would be her savior approaching her with the needle.

"No! Please . . . I just want to go home. You have no idea what I've been through," Breeze reasoned.

Ms. Beth ignored the pleas and jammed the needle painfully deep into Breeze's vein.

"Aghh!" Breeze cried out as blood trickled from her arm. She could feel the tension leave her body as a tear of defeat slipped from her eyes.

"What are you doing to me? What have you been giving me?" Breeze whispered as the orgasmic high once again came over her.

Ms. Beth looked cruelly back at her and smirked before replying, "Heroin. By the time I'm done with you, you will be nothing but a junkie whore."

Breeze's soul cried out silently as she felt herself going into a nod. The last thing she heard was Ms. Beth's voice.

"Shoot her up twice. She's going to be a handful. The faster we get her hooked the better. She'll learn to go with the flow one way or another."

Chapter Five

"Everything is easier if you forget about your past."
–*Liberty*

It was pitch black when Breeze finally came to, but she could hear the cries and groans of the other girls around her. The air was so thick that she could barely breathe, and her stomach rumbled violently as the urge to defecate overwhelmed her. She could smell the stench of bodily waste around her, and she gagged from the horrendous odor. She was sick partly from the stench and partly from her body craving its new best friend, heroin.

Breeze did not know how long she had been out, but she knew that Ms. Beth was transporting her somewhere. As she reached out her hands, she felt the steel walls. The bumpy road beneath her let her know that she was in the back of an industrial truck. The wails of the young women around her told her that she had been there for a while.

Her situation had just gone from bad to worse. She took deep breaths to stop herself from panicking, but it was no use. Breaking down was the only thing left for her to do. *I should have never trusted her*, Breeze thought as she withdrew into herself, curling up with her knees to her chest. She cried so hard that her chest hurt, and each time she gulped in air, she felt like she was suffocating. Unable to hold it in any longer, she threw up all over herself.

"It's easier if you breathe out of your mouth," she heard

a girl beside her say. "It won't smell as bad if you take it in through your mouth. Bring your face low near the seams of the wall. There's a little bit of fresh air down here. I have a small blanket you can breathe into."

Breeze huddled down near the girl and took a small piece of the fabric into her hands as she breathed into it. The girl's technique did not provide much relief, but it was better than nothing, and Breeze was grateful for it.

"Thanks," Breeze whispered.

"You're welcome. I'm Liberty," the girl stated.

"Breeze," she replied. No other words needed to spoken to establish a friendship. They took a liking to each other because they both realized that they were one and the same. Their fates were not their own, and their lives no longer theirs to live. As they clung to the blanket, they wrapped their arms around one another and prayed together. Neither of them knew what lay in store for them, but they were both terrified of the possibilities.

"How long have we been in this truck?" Breeze asked.

"I've seen the light come and go two times. Two full days have passed," Liberty replied, referring to the tiny bit of sunshine that crept through the crevice in the wall.

"Where are they taking us?" Breeze asked frightfully.

"They are taking us to Murderville," Liberty replied solemnly. "I am not new here. I've been there before, and it is worse than death."

Breeze did not respond, but her thoughts ran wild. She had seen the name MURDERVILLE scribbled in graffiti on Ms. Beth's boat, and now she hated herself for allowing the white woman to sell her a dream. She had been to a place that felt worse than death when she had been with Ma'tee, and now thanks to her naivety she was on her way right back to hell.

After seeing the sun rise and set one more day, Breeze felt

the truck finally stop moving. Hungry and soiled, she peeled herself off of the floor when the back door was lifted. She felt like cattle marching to slaughter as she was herded off of the truck. They were placed in a line side by side, and because she had no one else to turn to, Breeze grabbed Liberty's hand tightly. They barely knew one another, but at that moment, a new friend was better than facing the unknown alone.

"Take off all your clothing," a black man stated as he walked up and down the rows of girls. Breeze was reluctant, but everyone around her obediently began to disrobe.

"Undress," Liberty whispered urgently.

"What?" Breeze exclaimed. "No."

"Everything is easier if you forget about your past. Your place is here now. Just do as they say," Liberty warned.

Feeling as if she could not sink any lower, Breeze pulled off her clothes. The life and times of being a Diamond heir, her father's princess, were so far removed that it almost felt like she had never lived it. She could not believe that her life had come to this. Her father had kept her closely for most of her life. He had protected her and guarded her, but instead of helping her, his overprotection hindered her. It had made her vulnerable, and that vulnerability had led her to this place.

She was nothing like her brothers. She was weak. As she stood in the line, tears flowed freely down her dirty face, and she helplessly watched as the man grabbed a high-pressure hose and aimed it at her line. She closed her eyes as she was blasted with cold water like an animal. Through it all, she cried. Liberty held her hand while the little bit of Breeze Diamond that was left was washed away.

"Hold out your arms," the man stated when he finally put the hose down. Breeze already knew what that meant, and although her mind told her to protest, her body urged her to give in. It had been three full days since Ms. Beth had injected her with her last fix, and already her body was hooked. It craved the drug against Breeze's will, and instead of fighting it, Breeze gave up. If she was going to have to live like this, she may as well be numb to the pain.

Breeze clung to Liberty as if her life depended on it. Day in and day out they kept each other sane, until one fateful afternoon, Ms. Beth came to the camp where they were being kept. Whenever she came around, an eerie aura swept over the girls. She was the one who had manipulated most of them into coming to Murderville in the first place, so everyone feared her. She was the perfect example of the blue-eyed, blonde-haired devil, and Breeze hated her.

As the girls stood to their feet and waited for Ms. Beth to deliver their daily fix, the room was silent. It had not taken long for Breeze to become a full-blown addict, and her eyes widened in anticipation as she watched each girl get their turn before her.

As Ms. Beth administered the deadly drug, she separated the girls into two different groups. Some of the girls would be taken and groomed for wealthy buyers, but the unfortunate young women would stay in Murderville and work in the brothels. They would be contracted out for private parties and have their bodies sold to those who could afford it. The girls in this group would be common whores, and once they were used up to the point of no return, they would be executed and replaced. This was the group Ms. Beth put Breeze in, while Liberty was one of the lucky ones. She was taken away to be groomed for a high-priced auction.

With no one left to depend on but herself, Breeze submitted to the world of drugs and sex. She was taken to a house with ten other girls and dressed up in sexy garments. She was so high that everything was a blur as the madame of the brothel put makeup on her face and sprayed perfume all over her body.

Lazily, Breeze lay sprawled across the satin sheets as her first client entered the room. Just looking at her, no one would have ever pegged her for a junkie. The only thing that gave her away were the track marks underneath the sheer fabric of the negligee.

The man that lingered over her lusted over Breeze's beautiful appearance. Under no other circumstance would he ever be able to be with a woman of her beauty.

Breeze was so out of it that all she could do was lie there as the man had his way with her. It was something that she had gotten used to. She had never chosen to give herself away to any man. She didn't know what it was like to feel a man's gentle touch. Her womanhood was always taken away, and she was never in a position to say no.

Chapter Six

"Forever Miamor would sleep with the fishes."
—*Unknown*

Murder arrived in Miami on a commercial flight with hatred in his heart. He soaked up all of the information from the Murder Mamas about The Cartel and Miamor's worst enemy, Mecca. With a thirst for revenge and pictures of the entire Diamond family, he was ready to find what was left of Miamor and get at The Cartel. Murder's hands never stopped shaking throughout the whole flight, not because of nervousness or fear, but because of the itch to get at whoever had brought pain to Miamor.

Murder demanded that Robyn and Aries stay in L.A., so that he could work the way he did best—alone, strategically, and uninterrupted. They all hoped desperately that Murder would find Miamor alive, but deep in all of their hearts, they knew what was to be found.

Murder got his bags and headed to the curb to catch a cab. He was headed to the exact address that was left inside the box with Miamor's severed hand. Murder's heart hurt every time he thought about the pain and agony that Mecca had brought upon his favorite girl, Miamor. He carefully studied the picture that Robyn and Aries had given him of the heads of The Cartel. He could pick Mecca's face out of a sea of people. Although Murder had never seen Mecca face to face, he knew his every facial feature, and it was a face that would be etched in his mind forever.

Every time Murder thought about Miamor's angelic smile, he had to fight back tears while wishing she was in his arms. It was a love that was unexplainable. Although Miamor looked at Murder as a big brother, Murder looked at Miamor as much more. He knew that she was the love of his life, and he would never be able to win her over, because deep in his heart, he knew she was dead.

He pulled out a picture of Mecca that Miamor had taken while she was preparing to hit him, and he studied it once more. Murder's hands began to shake as he clenched his teeth so tightly that it seemed as if he would chip a tooth. Just as a driver pulled up on him, he stuck the photo in his inner jacket pocket and caught a cab to his hotel.

Mecca cruised through the Miami streets unable to focus on the road because he kept checking his rearview mirror. He suspected that the tinted minivan was following him for the past few blocks. "What the hell?" Mecca whispered as he glanced in the mirror again and saw that the van had made the same right turn that he did. Mecca, tired of playing the game of cat and mouse, reached under his seat to retrieve his automatic handgun. He smoothly placed it on his lap as he approached the upcoming yellow traffic light.

"Niggas trying to catch me slipping? Not today," he stated as he eased up to the light and made a complete stop. The van pulled up behind him, and that was when Mecca clicked on. His street instincts took over, and he acted on impulse. He threw the car into park and quickly hopped out of the car, gun in hand.

"Why the fuck are you following me?" Mecca yelled. He

had his gun gripped tightly, holding it like a professional marks-men, almost like a cop would do. Mecca quickly crept up to the car, not giving the driver time to make a move. When Mecca got a glimpse of the driver, he instantly felt silly.

A pregnant, blonde white woman was the only person in the car. She quickly threw both of her hands up and froze in utter terror as a pool of tears filled her eyes. She tried to scream, but Mecca was in her grill so quickly that she had no time to let out a sound. He waved the gun in her face through the open driver's side window.

Mecca saw the terrified look in the woman's face and in-stantly felt guilty. He knew that his nerves were making him reckless, and he made stupid choices when he was reckless. It was something that he was trying to change. His paranoia eased up. *Everybody's not out to get you*, Mecca thought as he regretted assaulting the soccer mom.

"Sorry, ma," Mecca said as he lowered his gun and took a deep breath. "You can go. I thought you were someone else," Mecca explained as he tried to give the woman a slight grin to ease the tension.

The woman still had her hands up and remained fearful as she stared into the eyes of a killer.

Mecca dropped his head and shook it from side to side as he lightly chuckled to himself. *I'm bugging the fuck out, spazzing on pregnant women and shit*, he thought to himself as he turned to head back to his car.

He began to think about the shadow of Estes that loomed over him. He knew that he would never be at peace until the beef with Estes was settled. He had to go to Estes and ask for his forgiveness. If he didn't, Mecca would always have to look over his shoulders, wondering when one of his grandfather's henchmen would kill him for what he had done to his twin brother.

Just as Mecca took the second step, he heard a familiar noise, which was that of a gun jamming. He quickly swung around and fired a bullet straight through the woman's neck. Mecca had underestimated Estes. He had killers on his team from all over, and the woman who he had thought was so innocent was really there to murder him.

She dropped the chrome .45 as her hands instinctively grabbed her neck. Blood gushed out of the hole like a faucet.

Mecca quickly stepped closer and let off another round, that time catching her in the forehead. Her head jerked back and she stared into space. Dead on impact.

Enraged, he lifted her shirt to reveal her bulging belly, only to find a pillow stuffed underneath. Estes was pulling out all the stops in the hunt for Mecca's head.

Mecca breathed hard as he held the gun tightly. He looked down and saw the gun in her lap. He knew that Estes' hired guns rarely missed, and if her gun had not jammed, he would be a dead man. Mecca gave her another shot to the chest for good measure as his temper flared from the rage he felt.

He was tired of running. He couldn't beef out with Estes. His grandfather's reach was too far, and Mecca knew that eventually he would lose. He paused, staring at her, knowing that he had almost been caught slipping.

"This shit has got to stop!" he yelled in frustration as he tucked his gun in his waistline and ran to his car, leaving the woman slumped in her seat.

Mecca sped off, filling the air with the sound of screeching tires. He knew exactly what he had to do in order to end the madness.

Murder stood at the front desk as he checked into the five-star hotel in Ft. Lauderdale. He wanted to observe from afar, and decided to stay in a suburban hotel instead of directly in the city, so that he could remain low key.

"Do I have a package waiting for me?" Murder asked as he gave the desk clerk a smile.

"Um, I don't know. Let me check," the young blonde said as she returned the smile to Murder. The desk clerk looked behind the counter and smiled as she saw the FedEx box addressed to the occupant of room 403, which was Murder's suite.

"Here we go, sir. It was dropped off this morning for a . . . Mr. M," she said as she glanced oddly at the box.

"Yeah, that's me. Thanks," he said as he slid his room key off the counter and grabbed the box. He headed for the elevators and hurried up to his suite.

Moments later, Murder ripped open the neatly packed box, retrieving two chrome 9 mm guns that Aries had sent to him. He loaded the clips and pulled out the piece of paper that had the address on it. He immediately placed the twin millies on his hip and headed out the door.

An hour later, a cab pulled outside of the brick house that sat on a small hill. Murder tipped the cabbie and watched as he left. Murder then looked at the house and took a deep breath. Murder began to second-guess his plan, and wondered if he was walking into a setup. He pulled out his guns and approached the house, going all out.

He approached the front door and turned the doorknob. It was unlocked, so he pushed the door open. He carefully stepped through the door with his gun drawn. The familiar smell of a rotting body overwhelmed him as he winced in displeasure. The horrendous stench was overbearing, and he instantly pulled his shirt over his nose.

Murder's heart began to thump as he got deeper into the empty house. The smell got heavier and heavier as he approached the door that led to the basement. He quickly snatched open the basement door and pointed his gun through the opening. The rotting smell had been magnified by ten when he opened the door. He held his breath as he began to walk down the stairs, preparing himself for what he was to find.

"Miamor, please don't let this be you," he whispered as his eyes got teary.

When Murder reached the bottom step, it felt as his heart had dropped into the pit of his stomach. He saw a decomposing corpse sprawled on the floor, hog-tied. He looked at the arm and noticed there was no hand attached to it. It was then that he knew that it was really Miamor. He instantly dropped to his knees and turned his head away, not wanting to see Miamor that way. Although he had known that finding her alive was unlikely, seeing her tortured and dismembered in the tomblike basement ripped his insides to pieces. The confirmation of her death was the only pain he had ever felt in his entire life. Murder was a cold soul, and before meeting Miamor, he didn't even think he was capable of love. But she had always been his weakness. She was the woman who could penetrate him, and now she was gone.

"No, ma . . . no," he whispered as he put his hand to his ears to drown out the sound of his own internal misery.

Murder's heart had just been broken in two. He had just verified that the world lost one of the realest bitches who ever walked it. The ultimate sin had been committed against her. It was about to be murder season in Miami. He didn't care if he had to make the entire city bleed. Somebody had to pay, and he was determined to get vengeance.

Murder, Aries, and Robyn sat on the fifty-foot yacht as they stared out at the Atlantic Ocean, all of them with pain in their hearts and revenge on their minds. Murder had sent for Robyn and Aries right after he found Miamor's body. They all knew that she was dead before Murder came to Miami, but they had to make sure. The vase full of ashes in their hands confirmed it: they had lost. They both had looked to Miamor as their leader. Her confidence made them confident, and now that she had been touched, they felt extremely vulnerable. Even though the sun was shining, it was a very cold day for Murder and the Murder Mamas.

"I'ma make sure all them niggas pay for what they did to Miamor," Murder mumbled as he shook his head from side to side and kept visualizing Miamor's beautiful smile.

"I know Mecca did this. He is sick in the head, and the only person twisted enough to do something like this. That crazy mu'fucka is the only one who would go to this extreme to do this to her," Robyn said as she held her lips tight.

"Yeah, Mecca did this to she," Aries whispered in her heavy accent as she shook her head in sadness.

"I'ma avenge Miamor's death for sure. These south niggas don't know how I get down. They ain't seen a nigga like me before," Murder said through his clenched teeth.

Robyn shook her head in disagreement. "It's not that simple, Murder. This shit is real. We've been hitting niggas for years, and we have never encountered any organization like theirs. They killed Anisa and Miamor. That shit don't happen to us. We were untouchable until we faced them. They are not like regular niggas. We are fucking with The Cartel, and they're not like these ol' corny clique-naming-ass niggas. Their shit is legit. I'm talking the best security, crazy gun power, and not to mention the entire fucking city rocks with them.

"If they move like they used to, it's hard to catch them together all at once. We tried to kill them one at a time, and that plan only backfired on us. I know how you get down, but you're only one man. You'll be going against a thousand niggas just as grimy as you are.

"This time, don't even give them a chance to hit back. You can't kill one; you have to kill them all. If you want to get them and do it right, you have to infiltrate their organization. You have to get close and go from the inside out," Robyn said, thinking about how they failed at every attempt to take down The Cartel using other tactics.

"Fuck that! I'ma do this my way," Murder said as his trigger finger began to itch.

"No, Murder. Chu have to listen to Robyn. You are going to be next if you go in blazing. Me no want to see no more dying. If anybody is going to be put in the dirt, let it be someone from the other side. Trust us. Please just do it our way," Aries pleaded as she looked into Murder's bloodshot eyes.

Robyn placed her hand on Murder's shoulder and looked in his eyes. She noticed the burning desire for revenge, and she had to let Murder know that he was dealing with a different breed when it came to The Cartel. "Murder, these niggas not playing. If you kill one, they are going to come and kill ten of yours. That's how they operate, so you have to do this thing right. You have to get in good with them and find out a way to kill them all at once. That way, you can dismantle them from the top. Kill the head, and the body will fall. Trust me!" Robyn said as a tear dropped as she thought of Miamor.

Murder nodded his head, giving in to her. He was willing to do whatever it took to take down The Cartel.

"We are going to get these niggas back," Robyn said as she quickly wiped the tear away and looked into the waves bouncing on top of the massive body of water.

"I want to do this one alone. The best way to do something is to do it solo. That's how I work," Murder said as he dropped his head and shook it from side to side. He then looked over at Aries and said, "Let's get this over with."

Aries opened the urn that had Miamor's remains in it. They decided to have her cremated because there was no way that she could have a funeral. Mecca had cut her up in four different pieces to prevent any hopes of a traditional open casket ceremony. Aries took a deep breath, glancing at Robyn and then Murder before she dropped a tear and released the ashes into the ocean. Forever Miamor would sleep with the fishes.

Chapter Seven

"Even family will betray you."
–*Garza*

Carter may have been locked up, but he wasn't dead, and in any circumstance, his survival instincts always kicked in. He was a hustler and could sell whatever, whenever, wherever, and prison was no exception. He knew of the weakened state that The Cartel was in, and he did not want to depend on anyone to keep him afloat, so although they had trapped his body, the feds could not contain his hustle. They had taken him off of the streets, but he had brought the streets to him.

He easily brought his product into the prison, and now he was running a lucrative heroin operation while locked up. The one thing that the game had taught him was that everybody loved money, and as long as everyone ate, things ran smoothly. Using a bitch as a mule was a sure way to get caught, so instead, he put correctional officers on his payroll. They brought it into the prison for him, and Zyir ensured that they were compensated properly with an anonymous wire transfer into each of their personal bank accounts. The guards were making more money working for Carter than they did on their day jobs, which made them compliant with all of his requests.

Carter wasn't flashy, however. He got money low key, keeping just enough to keep his books full, and then had the rest delivered to Zyir, who was putting it toward his case. He kept to himself, and spent his time reading books. He knew that the only person who truly cared about his freedom was himself, so he educated himself on the law so that the system would not be able to jam him up. He refused to let the feds lock him up and throw away the key.

As he sat silently on his bed, he peeked up at his cellmate. He knew that the Mexican cat did not like him, and the feeling was mutual. Carter would much rather be in a cell alone, but the overcrowding issues of the prison made it nearly impossible. The two never spoke. They kept a respectable distance from one another, always keeping their interactions to the bare minimum. They were a part of two different worlds, and because they had respect for the game that they both played, they had established an unspoken truce. What Carter did not know was that Garza had been watching him, and he had the power to offer Carter what he desperately craved—his freedom.

Carter sat alone at his table in the cafeteria as he ate silently. Although other members of The Cartel were incarcerated with him, he felt no need to be friendly. They were there for his protection and only his protection. He didn't need another man to keep him company; his thoughts were enough. Miamor plagued his mind, as did the current state of The Cartel. They needed a plug and needed it bad. The low quality heroin he was running through the prison was not potent enough for his outside dealings. Scarcity made it acceptable inside the walls, but on the outside, it was a completely different game. Zyir and Mecca were grasping at straws trying to secure other connects, but nobody was willing to mess with them. Everyone was afraid of the repercussions of being associated with The Cartel. He was carrying huge burdens on his shoulders, and being locked up made him feel powerless. Detaching himself from the outside would be the only way that he would become accustomed to prison, but with Zyir, Mecca, and the responsibilities that came with being the leader of The Cartel it was hard to block it out.

As Carter ate, he watched an inmate approach his table. Carter continued to eat, unfazed as one of the members of The Cartel got up from the table next to him. His goons were never out of arm's reach.

"Hold up, homeboy," the loyal affiliate stated as he stopped the inmate in his tracks.

"Yo, I'm not on no beef shit. I know better than to beef with this man. I just came to rap with him for a second," the inmate stated as he pulled a carton of cigarettes out of the top of his jail jumpsuit. The cigarettes were a sign of respect. In prison, money did not come easy, so the fact that the little nigga had spent a nice chunk of his commissary on them bought him a moment of Carter's time.

Carter's goon looked at him for approval, and Carter nodded his head for him to let the boy pass. The goon patted the inmate down for good measure to ensure that the visit really was a friendly one.

"Carter, I've heard a lot about you, and I just wanted to personally introduce myself. I'm from Opa-Locka, and when I was on the outside, I was doing my thing thing, you know?" he stated as he clapped his hands together. "I know that's your territory and all, 'cause you sent the young goon Zyir through to shut my shit down. I wanted to let you know ain't no hard feelings or nothing on my end, but I am trying to get on board with your movement. I'm outta here in a few months, and I don't got nothing to go home to. Like, nothing, fam. So when I say I'm hungry, I mean it. I don't want to make the mistake of stepping on your toes again, so I wanted to know what I have to do to get down. I'll put in work any way you need me to," the guy finished.

Carter continued to eat and didn't even look up as he said, "What did you say your name was?"

"Ibrahim," the guy replied.

Carter took his time and gathered his thoughts before he spoke. The uncomfortable silence between the two men made the inmate shift nervously from side to side.

Finally, Carter looked up at the dude. "Sit down, my man. Everybody don't need to hear what I'm about to say."

Feeling as if Carter was about to put him on, the guy smiled as he took a seat across from the hood legend. Carter's name indeed rang bells in and out of prison. Anyone in the game knew exactly who he was.

"You said my li'l man Zyir shut your shit down?" Carter asked.

The dude nodded and replied, "Yeah, he told me I was out of bounds. That those blocks were already spoken for."

"And what did you do to handle that situation?" Carter asked.

"I didn't mean no disrespect, fam. I moved my operation to a different block," he replied.

"See, that's where my problem lies, Ibrahim. Do you think I got where I am by letting other niggas run me off the block?" Carter asked. "Now, if you had blazed on my li'l nigga, maybe then we would have something to talk about. That would have showed me you had heart, but you didn't. You let another man, who bleeds just like you bleed, stop you from getting money. I can't afford to have any weak links in my chain, Ibrahim."

With that said, Carter resumed his meal as he waited for Ibrahim to dismiss himself. The conversation was over, but Carter knew there would be more to come. Many men had approached him since he had been locked up, and it was always the same story. Everybody wanted to be put on, but Carter didn't rock with new niggas. He knew that if he let too many people into his circle, it would not seem exclusive. Everybody in the hood wanted to be a part of something, but unfortunately, not many fit the bill to be a member of The Cartel. Carter definitely had no use for a scary nigga. He only wanted the elite.

The inmate nodded his head, his ego slightly bruised as he stood to his feet. He slowly slid the cigarette carton over to Carter.

"For your time," he said respectfully.

Carter nodded his head and stood to his feet as he headed back to his cell. He handed the carton to Garza as soon as he entered. Carter didn't smoke cigarettes, and although he never spoke to his cellmate, he always passed the unwanted gifts along to him.

"How did you end up in here?" Garza asked. Carter looked up in surprise. They had never engaged one another before, so the question was completely unexpected.

"An associate of mine found himself on the wrong side of the law. It was a person who I thought I could trust, someone who I grew up with. He was like family."

"Even family will betray you," Garza interrupted as he lit a smoke.

"So I learned," Carter replied with a chuckle. The situation was comical to him. He had done nothing but show Ace love, but the first chance Ace got, he had stabbed him in the back—and plunged the blade deep. Carter knew that once Ace took the stand and testified against him, that it would be all the jury needed to hear to convict him.

"I've been watching you, observing how you move. I've seen how the men in here treat you," Garza replied. "Even the guards march to the beat of your drum. It would be a shame to see a man of your talents end up in here because of a snake. It seems that your problem could be handled if you knew who to ask for help."

"I don't ask for help. Anything that I can't do on my own is not worth doing. I've never owed anyone anything a day in my life," Carter stated surely. He did not know what Garza was getting at, but already he did not like the sound of it.

"That is the problem with your kind."

"There's not another man like me. I don't have a kind," Carter interrupted sternly.

"I do not mean any disrespect, but the Blacks don't know how to form alliances. Someone with your mentality could be very valuable. The way that you move product is a skill that not many people have. The power you have over others is rare as well. I've done my research on you and The Cartel. If you are willing to extend a hand of friendship, I know some people who can help you out of your predicament."

Carter's interest was piqued. "Nobody does anything for free."

"A partnership between the Diamond Cartel and the Garza Cartel would be payment enough. We have the product that you need, and you have the influence that we need in the South. Together we would be unstoppable."

"Until one party becomes envious of the other," Carter protested.

The old man shook his head as he continued to smoke. "That will never become a problem for us. I can guarantee that my people are not in it for the limelight, only the money. As long as the money is correct, there will not be a problem. This could be a beautiful thing if you are willing to expand your horizons."

"I don't work underneath others," Carter insisted.

"Not under others, Carter, with others. There is a difference. Working with my people, your reach will be limitless. Mexico is not like the United States. In my country, we are above the law," Garza explained.

"Why are you still in here? If it is so easy to make my case disappear, why not do the same for yourself?" Carter asked. Although the deal was appealing, he was skeptical to trust Garza's word too quickly. He wanted to cover all of his bases.

"I chose my own destiny. I'm an old man. An organization of my family's magnitude leaves a lot of bodies in its path. Someone has to be held accountable for those. I took responsibility because I saw the bigger picture. I'm in here for twenty different counts of confessed murder. I have lived my life and done my part so that my family's reign could go on. What I'm offering you is a deal too sweet for any man to refuse."

Garza extended his hand, and Carter reluctantly accepted. "Nothing will be set in stone until a face to face is held. I'll send my right hand, Zyir, to meet with your people," Carter stated.

"I will phone home tomorrow to let my brother Felipe know to expect him. This will be a beautiful thing for everyone involved."

"Only time will tell," Carter responded. He knew that getting in bed with the Mexican drug cartel could prove very wise. He just had to ensure that everyone understood the terms of the agreement, because if something went wrong, Carter was almost certain that The Cartel would not be able to withstand another war.

Mecca could not take it anymore. Watching his back every second of every day was becoming too much to bear. He knew that there was only one way to dead his beef with Estes. He had to go see his grandfather. The same man who had sent the killers to his front door was the only one who could call them off. He hoped that he could reason with Estes and that he would remember that Monroe was not his only grandson.

He had made a mistake by killing Monroe, and it was a regret that he would live with for the rest of his life. Estes' vengeance was not necessary. The burden was already heavy enough, sometimes too heavy for him to carry.

As Mecca ventured on his grandfather's side of town, his instincts sharpened. He kept his eyes in his rearview and one hand on his pistol. He never wanted to be caught slipping again, so he stayed ready, safety off. It would be the wrong day to run up on him unannounced. He knew that he would never make it through his grandfather's door with a gun, so he hoped that Estes did not have him killed on sight.

Mecca had love for no one besides family. He remembered the Christmas holidays and the many birthdays that had been spent in his grandfather's presence. How long ago that seemed now. How easily they both had forgotten.

It seemed to Mecca that Estes placed more value on his relationship with Monroe. The little boy that respected his grandfather simply wanted to be loved, but the grown, cold man that Mecca had come to be wanted to place his grandfather in the dirt.

As he finally neared Estes' home, he parked at the public beach and decided to walk along the sand behind his grandfather's house. The fact that Estes' house sat directly on the water helped Mecca go undetected. The many people that were enjoying the sun allowed him to blend in, and as he neared his grandfather's home, he noticed that Estes was outside sitting on his patio. A few feet away from him, a woman stood in a sundress and large sunhat, holding a child in her arms. Estes seemed to be distracted by the woman's presence as Mecca approached.

He wished that he had brought his pistol with him. It was the first time he had seen his grandfather so relaxed. There were no bodyguards in sight, and it would have been the perfect time to end their beef once and for all, but Mecca knew that he did not have time to go back to his car. He had to try to reason with Estes.

Mecca watched the woman go inside, and Estes' eyes were so focused on the woman that he never saw Mecca walk up.

"Hello, Grandfather," Mecca greeted in a low, steady tone.

Caught completely off guard, Estes turned around to find Mecca standing before him. He half expected to be shot instantly. Mecca lifted his arms and shirt and then said, "I'm not strapped."

"Why not? I would not have extended you the same courtesy," Estes replied as he pulled a .45 from underneath the table. It had been resting in his lap, but Estes immediately showed his cards to let Mecca know that he was constantly aware of the business he was in.

"You're still alive," Estes observed as his eyes roamed his grandson cautiously, surveying him to see if he was injured.

"Diamonds are forever," Mecca replied.

"Tell that to your brother," Estes shot back. He clicked off his safety as his finger gripped the trigger of his gun. "You're a snake, Mecca. You're a traitor. You killed my grandson."

"Am I not your grandson, Estes?" Mecca asked.

Estes fixed his mouth to respond, but was interrupted when Leena emerged from the house with her son in one arm and a bowl of fruit in her hands. She was so busy trying to balance everything without dropping it that she didn't look up. When she finally did, both she and Mecca got the surprise of their lives.

"Leena?"

Her name fell out of his mouth without him even knowing it, and the sound of his voice caused her to drop the glass bowl in her hands, causing tiny glass fragments to explode on the ground. Her heart beat in fear as she instinctively gripped her son in protection.

Mecca's eyes widened as if he were seeing a ghost. He had shot her himself. For all this time, he had thought that she was dead. Now here she was, standing before him, as beautiful as he remembered. His gaze went from her to the child in her arms. He looked like a tiny replica of Mecca, but deep in his heart, Mecca knew that the little boy was not his seed. Mecca was sterile, and the child in Leena's arm was his nephew. It was Money's son, and that fact brought the betrayal that he had felt rushing back to him.

Tears came to Leena's eyes as she saw Mecca's expression go from sad to angry. She knew him, and felt as if he would explode at any moment. Estes didn't hesitate to chamber a bullet in his gun. He, too, recognized the look in his grandson's eyes.

"It's that easy for you to shoot me, Estes? Your flesh and blood," Mecca stated as he looked back and forth between Lena and Estes. Seeing her reminded him of his sins, and his bottom lip began to quiver uncontrollably. He held his arms out at his sides as Estes' finger rested on the trigger. "Did Money mean that much more? Why is his life more valuable than mine? Huh, Estes? Why does everybody hate Mecca?"

Estes was silent but unflinching as he listened to Mecca break down. "Ever since we were little, everybody always favored Money. Mecca was the bad twin. I was the unwanted seed! My heart was cold before the streets ever got a hold of me. Everybody always loved Money . . . never me," Mecca shouted, getting years of pent-up emotion off of his chest.

His words brought tears to Leena's eyes, because even she had chosen Monroe over Mecca. She had contributed to his hurt, to his isolation.

"There is no excuse," Estes spoke up, unaffected by Mecca's outburst. "You murdered your brother. You knew what the consequences would be for your actions. Be a man and take what you deserve," Estes said without the theatrics. He was calm and sure of his decision as he raised his gun, aiming it at Mecca's heart. Just as he was about to pull the trigger, Leena stopped him.

"Emilio, please don't," Leena whispered. She couldn't take her eyes off of Mecca as her tears began to flow. "There has been enough bloodshed." Her voice was pleading, and even though she hated Mecca, she did not want to see him dead. He looked so much like Monroe, like her son, and as she read the hurt in his stare, she began to think about Mecca's pain for the first time since she had been shot.

"Leena?" Mecca repeated in disbelief as he stumbled backward a bit, completely in shock.

Estes stood to his feet and stepped close to Mecca. His gun hung threateningly in his palm. "She just saved your life, son. You are no grandson of mine. You will keep your distance," Estes said. He did not raise his voice, but his tone was all the warning that Mecca needed.

"What do I have to do to get your forgiveness, Estes?" Mecca whispered so that only the two of them could hear his plea.

"Ask God for forgiveness. I have none to give," Estes replied.

Mecca stepped back and wiped his face with one hand. "You'll call off your dogs," Mecca countered.

Estes looked back at Leena, who nodded her head as she wiped the tears away while holding her son tightly.

Estes replied dryly, "I will."

Mecca extended his hand to his grandfather, but Estes walked away disgusted. He had no respect for Mecca, and did not want there to be any misunderstandings. Estes would never welcome Mecca back into his family.

Mecca walked away stunned. His mind was completely blown. The mixed emotions that Mecca felt threw him completely off balance. Seeing Leena alive and healthy, seeing her breathing, had taken his mind back to when everything was as it should be. She reminded him of the days that were so carefree, and the baby boy that mirrored him in image made him think of Monroe. He wanted to think that the fresh little man he had just seen was his own son, but he knew better. It wasn't even possible for Mecca to procreate. He was shooting blanks. It was as if God knew that nothing good could ever come from him.

Leena had given birth to his nephew and had been in hiding, living with Estes all this time. Now that he had seen her, he did not know if he could just walk away. Her affair with his flesh and blood had led Mecca to kill his own twin. Her survival enraged him, while at the same time, it pleased him. He had so many questions that only she could answer.

How long had she and Monroe been fucking? Why did she choose him over me? What the fuck is she doing with Estes? Mecca thought as he sauntered blankly down the sandy beach. These things burned in his mind, and he knew that he would not be satisfied until he got some answers. He got into his car and pulled away, knowing that he would not stay away for long.

Leena watched from the upstairs window as Mecca disappeared up the beach. Fear paralyzed her as she thought of what he might do now that he knew of her existence. Seeing him again terrified her, but when she had looked in his eyes, her heart felt like it would beat out of her chest.

Mecca symbolized so many things in her life. He looked as if he had been through so much anguish since the last time she saw him. He had aged, matured, changed, and she did not know if it was for the better. She saw misery in his stare, and his features were so identical to Monroe's that she could not help but fall in love at first sight.

She did not know how two brothers who were so physically alike could be so different on the inside. She hoped that Mecca would let her be. She had pieced her life back together seamlessly with the help of Estes, and the last thing she needed was another Diamond brother to come along and tear her world apart.

"Are you okay?"

Leena released Mecca from her gaze as she turned around at the sound of Estes' voice. She nodded unsurely as she put on a phony smile. "I'm fine," she replied.

Estes came over to her and removed baby Monroe from her arms. The one year old went to him happily. Estes was the only man that had ever been around her son. He was the only stability in her life, but seeing Mecca had been like a bad omen, and she felt it in her bones that a deadly storm was about to blow her way.

Chapter Eight

"A real live American boy."
–*Illiana*

When Zyir stepped off of the private plane, the overwhelming heat hit him instantly. His baggy khaki shorts and white button-down linen shirt seemed too heavy for the Mexican heat. He unbuttoned his shirt, revealing the crisp white wife beater underneath. His eyes were hidden behind the Homme shades he wore.

The hidden airstrip that they had used to fly in on was undetected by the Mexican government, so Zyir felt secure as he stepped off of the plane. Still, he knew that because his presence in Mexico was completely undetected, if something were to happen to him, no one would even know where to begin looking.

He had wanted to bring Mecca along, because that was the one person he knew would not be afraid to pop off if things got out of hand, but Mecca was a hot head, and could easily blow this deal for them. Because of this, Carter had insisted that Zyir go alone, and even though he went everywhere strapped, he felt that it would be of little use in the foreign country.

"*Buenas tardes, señor,*" the driver greeted as he held open the limousine door.

Zyir nodded his head to greet the man, and then stepped

inside of the plush vehicle. A full liquor bar was set up for him inside, but he chose not to partake. He was there to handle business only. He could bullshit back home.

He attempted to keep his bearings as the limo took him to his destination, but he quickly realized that it was no use. He did not know where he was being escorted, and the fact that he was not in control pushed him out of his comfort zone. Trust would be his only way of getting through this meeting. He would have to hope that the men he was about to meet with were men of honor. If not, he was about to walk into a situation where he was greatly outnumbered.

Zyir watched as the city turned into countryside as they drove along the coastline. An hour later, they pulled up to an estate much grander than anything he had ever seen. The beauty of it was magnificent. He admired the stone exterior. He was brought back to reality, however, when he noticed the armed guards standing post at the gates and aiming their automatic sniper rifles from their high towers. The property was guarded like a fort.

Zyir's palms began to sweat as he attempted to keep his composure. He removed his pistol and placed it underneath the seat of the limo. He knew that the sixteen bullets from his 9 mm would be no match for the artillery that the guards were equipped with. They would fill him with holes before he even let off a shot. So, he was making the first effort to establish a trusting alliance with the Mexicans by going in unarmed. It was his way of showing good faith.

The guards peered into the car, and once Zyir's identity was confirmed, he was admitted onto the property.

The atmosphere was not what he had assumed it would be. There were no bikini clad women and no sleazy lifestyle taking place. It reminded him of the Diamond estate. It was a family home, and he relaxed a bit when he stepped out of the car.

"Welcome to Mexico, Zyir," a man greeted as he emerged from the mansion.

"You must be Felipe," Zyir responded. "I appreciate the invitation. We have a lot to discuss."

"That we do, but my wife has prepared a beautiful lunch for you on the back terrace. Let's eat first. The time for business will come soon," Felipe stated. He led Zyir through the home and out onto the back terrace that faced the ocean.

"Zyir, this is my wife, Maria, and my sister Illiana," Felipe introduced.

"Very nice to meet you, Zyir," Maria greeted.

"A real live American boy," Illiana stated as she surveyed Zyir, her dark, mischievous eyes looking him up and down as she sipped on a cocktail.

Her dark hair and striking features immediately stood out to Zyir. He had never seen a woman so beautiful. As she stared him down, Zyir knew that there was nothing good about this girl. She was a temptress, and the deep pools that were her eyes were hypnotic. He quickly broke their stare to avoid becoming lost in them.

She was the most exotic young woman he had ever seen. She exuded a confidence and sexiness that he had never encountered before. Zyir was no fool, however. He knew that to do business with the Garza family meant that Illiana would be the forbidden fruit. Wars had been sparked over women, and no matter how exotic she appeared, no pussy was that good. He was always about his dollar.

Not wanting to appear too friendly, Zyir nodded his acknowledgements and took a seat. It was customary for a wife to welcome the guests of her husband, and Maria ensured that Zyir was comfortable. The four ate and spoke as if they were old acquaintances, but Zyir was simply being polite and going through the motions. He was itching to get to the money, but knew that he had to build a rapport before Felipe would even bring it up.

Although there were only four people at the table, Zyir was well aware that he was being evaluated by many more. After much unwanted banter, Zyir finally spoke up. His patience was running real low. *I'm not here on a social call,* he thought. *If we ain't talking money, then we're wasting time.*

He leaned into Felipe so that the women could not overhear and said, "I'm ready to get down to it. I appreciate your hospitality, but it really isn't necessary. Time is of the essence, nah mean?"

Felipe put his hand on Zyir's shoulder. "My man . . . in such a rush. Sometimes you have to do things slowly in order to do them efficiently, my friend," he replied. He stared tensely at Zyir, and then snapped his fingers, making one of his housekeepers rush quickly to his side.

"*¿Sí, señor?*" the elderly woman asked.

"Rosa, please take my friend's glass and get him a fresh drink," Felipe instructed.

Zyir never broke Felipe's stare, because there was not a man on this earth who could intimidate him. He was fearless as he sat, one man against what he was sure was an entire Mexican army lingering in the shadows of the massive estate. It was clear that Felipe held the power, and by making Zyir wait, he was sending a clear message that everyone on the southern side of the border moved at the pace of the Garza family, including Zyir.

Illiana watched Zyir's interaction with her brother and secretly admired him. In no form was Zyir bowing to Felipe, and his demeanor intrigued her. She was not used to opposition. No one ever had the balls to hold their ground against the Garza Cartel, but it was obvious that the reputation was not impressive to Zyir.

The housekeeper came back with a new drink for Zyir and then turned to Felipe and announced, "It has been done, señor. He is not in the database."

Felipe's mood immediately changed, and his callous expression transformed into a satisfied smile. "I apologize, Zyir. I had to make sure that you are who you say you are. I lifted your prints off of your cocktail glass and had one of my men run them through your country's national federal database. All federal agents must have their prints taken. A man in my position can never be too cautious," Felipe explained.

Not wanting to appear too impressed, Zyir held his cards, but he was inwardly pleased at how thorough Felipe was. "I understand," Zyir replied.

"Now, if you two will excuse us," Felipe stated as he stood to his feet. "I think I have wasted enough of this man's time."

"Surely lunch with me was not a waste of time," Illiana spoke up, seduction oozing off of her words.

Zyir smirked and then followed Felipe into the mansion.

By the time Zyir departed Mexico, he had secured a new connect and partnership with Felipe. The Cartel was back on, and with the pull that the Garza Cartel possessed, it was only a matter of time before Carter was free and money flowed again.

As Ace stared out of the hotel window, he could not believe his life had come to this. Hiding out in northern Pennsylvania with no contact to the outside world was not what he called a life. Foolishly, he had tried to backdoor The Cartel and sell bricks of cocaine on the side. He had gotten greedy. Tired of constantly working beneath Carter, he had tried to expand on his own, but there was a reason why Carter kept him in the background of the operation. Ace did not have the makings of a boss, and he proved that when he sold a kilo of coke to an undercover federal agent. The feds could almost smell the fear on Ace, and they took advantage of it from the very beginning. Once Ace revealed his connection to The Cartel, he became a pawn in their game to take down Carter, and like a true snitch-ass nigga, Ace obliged to save his own behind.

The life of a federal witness was not what he anticipated. He was forced to go into hiding until the end of the trial, and the detachment he felt knowing that he had turned on his former best friend ate at him. He was set to testify in court in two weeks, but the closer the date came, the more he wanted to change his story. He knew that things could never go back to the way they used to be, but he had come up from the gutter with Carter, and he knew that if the shoe was on the other foot, Carter would have never betrayed him.

Ostracized from everyone he loved and knew, Ace was living a lonely existence. At least in prison he would still have his family. If he had lived by the code of the streets and stayed true to the game, he would have been able to hold his head up high. He was a man, and no one had forced him to play the game the way he had. In his heart, he knew that he had no honor, and that he was causing the demise of another black man. He wanted to recant the statements that he had made to the feds, but he knew it was too late.

Even if he took everything back, the hood would know that he had flipped on Carter, and they would never forget. The streets had no love for snitches, and he was already a marked man. His only option was to testify and then disappear in the witness protection program. It was his only way to start over and begin a new life.

When we started in the game, neither of us ever thought it would turn out like this, he thought solemnly as he reminisced over his early days hustling with Young Carter.

A knock at the door interrupted his reverie as one of the federal agents entered the room. They were his protection, the only barrier between him and the ruthless team of killers that he was sure Carter had ordered to find him. Ace was sure that Mecca was among the wolves coming for his head. Ace only hoped that they never found him. This was how he would live the remainder of his days, looking over his shoulder every second of every hour as the paranoia ate away at his existence.

"Here's your food," the agent stated as he wheeled in a silver covered platter.

"Thanks," Ace stated as he sat down to eat his meal alone. Halfway through his meal, he grasped his throat in horror as he felt his airway become constricted. He attempted to yell out in distress as his eyes widened and he struggled to breathe. He stood frantically, knocking the table on its side as he flailed around the room, gasping for air. Sweat poured from his brow as his insides burned.

The federal agents burst into the room to find their key witness on the ground. His bloodshot eyes pleaded for them to call for help.

"Call a bus!" one of the agents shouted as he bent over to check Ace's pulse. He looked at the food on the floor and concluded. "Secure the cooking staff downstairs. It's the food! He's been poisoned!"

Ace felt himself slipping in and out of consciousness as the agents rushed into action around him. The paramedics finally arrived on the scene and lifted his convulsing body onto a gurney.

"Please . . . help," Ace managed to squeeze out.

"We are going to take care of you, sir," the paramedic stated. "Try to focus on me. Stay with me. You're going to be okay."

Ace focused on the sound of the paramedic's voice as he was loaded into the back of the ambulance. The man's words reassured him, but he knew that this would only be the first attempt of many on his life. The Cartel had failed this time— fortunately for him, the federal agents had gotten him help in just the nick of time— but they would not always be around to protect him, and now that his location was known, Ace was more fearful than ever before.

The ambulance sped recklessly through traffic as it rushed him to the hospital. Ace closed his eyes to conserve his energy. It wasn't until he felt the electric bolts pulsing through his body that he realized something was wrong.

"Aghhh!" He yelled as the paramedics shocked him. The voltage was up so high that the hair on his bare chest smoked. "Fuck is going on?"

Before he realized what was happening, he watched the Mexican man place a gun in the center of his forehead. He did not recognize the men, and the look of confusion was apparent on his face. The ambulance stopped moving, and the back doors were snatched open. He looked up and into the face of the devil—Mecca Diamond. Next to him stood a stoic Zyir.

Felipe's soldiers removed their paramedic disguises and hopped out as Mecca and Zyir climbed in.

Ace attempted to sit up, but was laid back down by the butt of Zyir's gun as it cracked the bridge of his nose.

"Zy, man . . . come on. We're family. I swear I won't say shit, fam. You don't have to do this," Ace begged as he reached out his hand toward Zyir.

Mecca scoffed in disgust. "This ol' pussy-ass nigga. Where the fuck Carter get this mu'fucka from?" he asked as he aimed his .357 and blew a hole through Ace's pleading hand.

"Aghh! Fuck!" Ace yelled in excruciating pain as blood spewed from his wound. He held his injured hand.

Ace knew that there would be no reasoning with Mecca, so

he hoped that Zyir would show him sympathy. "Zyir, we came in this together."

"And you going out alone, my nigga," Zyir stated coldly. His loyalty was to Carter. Any love that he had for Ace had dissipated when Ace turned snitch. Zyir figured that if Ace was willing to turn Carter in, it would only be a matter of time before his own name turned up on a federal affidavit.

Tired of the "remember the times" love song that Ace was singing, Mecca emptied his clip into Ace, silencing him forever. Zyir then walked around to the driver's seat and put the vehicle in drive. He and Mecca stood as they watched the ambulance roll through the highway rails and plunge down into the mountainous valleys below.

They turned around and shook hands with Felipe's men. Their connection with the Garza Cartel was already proving to be valuable. It was Felipe who had located Ace, and because of him, at that very moment, the federal judge presiding over Carter's case was being paid off handsomely. Without Ace, the feds' case would be too weak to convict, and when Carter's lawyer requested a dismissal, the judge would oblige.

Chapter Nine

"Yeah, I know you're a Diamond, Mecca. Me and everybody else in Miami knows!"
—*Leena*

Making the trip to Mexico the second time was bittersweet for Zyir. He was eager to begin their business relationship with the Garza Cartel, but he was upset by the fact that he missed Carter's last day in trial. He would soon have his freedom, and Zyir wanted to be there to congratulate him when he walked out of the prison walls. He knew that his task in Mexico was more important, however. Carter had groomed him well, and he knew that above all else, the money was always first priority. They could celebrate later. Today, Zyir had three tons of cocaine to pick up. Nobody dealt in quantities that large, and with that much access to the product, it was only a matter of time before they were the largest drug cartel in the nation. Miami was only the beginning.

When Zyir pulled up to the Garza estate this time, there was no hesitation. He had already established a level of trust with Felipe, and was granted access with ease. He was greeted by Felipe, who stood waiting with open arms.

"Zyir, my friend," Felipe said as the two men embraced briefly. "I have something to show you."

Zyir followed Felipe around to the back of the estate, until they came upon two Mack trucks.

Felipe pulled up the back of one of the semi-trucks, and his eyes widened as he took in the beautiful sight before him: rows and rows of neatly packed kilos. There were so many bricks that they gave off a sparkle. Zyir had never seen so much work in his life, and the sight made his hands itch, because he knew that soon a lot of money was going to flow.

"There are three tons between the two trucks. I have the entire first shift of border patrol on payroll. You and your people will be able to drive straight through without being stopped," Felipe stated.

Zyir quickly added up the total worth of the cocaine in his head. Three tons equaled three thousand bricks. They would easily go for twenty-five a pop, and even after splitting the take with Felipe, The Cartel stood to profit almost $40 million. It was a big payday for everyone, and as long as everything went flawlessly, there were many more lucrative deals to come in the future.

"Cat got your tongue, Zyir?"

Zyir turned around and saw Illiana standing behind him. Her tanned skin glowed flawlessly, and she hid her mysterious eyes behind large Dior sunglasses. Her voluptuous body was displayed in the designer two-piece bikini and matching cover-up she wore. Every part of her appeared perfect as Zyir took a quick glance, admiring her top to bottom, taking in everything from her pedicured feet to the seductress red stain on her lips. "Illiana," he acknowledged. He kissed her cheek quickly before turning his attention back to the task at hand.

Felipe put his arm around Zyir. The gesture was too friendly for Zyir, and he had to bite his tongue quickly so that he did not react. He had never let another man "son" him in his life, and although he was young in age, he was wise in years, something that Felipe would learn in time.

"I am aware of The Cartel's recent financial troubles, so I

am willing to extend these kilos on consignment. However, this is too large of an order for me to just entrust them to you. I'd like to send one of my people to Miami with you to watch over my investment," Felipe stated.

"That won't be a problem," Zyir replied. "We fully understand your position, and Carter extends his assurance that this partnership will be beneficial for all involved."

"I'll have to meet this Carter. My brother Garza speaks highly of him. After his legal affairs are handled, I would like to invite the two of you back down here. No business . . . just a meeting among men. I'll have to show the two of you a good time."

"I'll be sure to extend the invitation," Zyir answered. "Who will you be sending to Miami?"

"Illiana," Felipe replied.

Zyir stopped walking mid-stride, as if he had heard Felipe wrong. "Illiana?"

"She will not get in your way. She will simply be my eyes and ears. I hope that you will put her up temporarily," Felipe suggested.

Zyir looked back at the seductive Illiana. He knew that her presence would only mean trouble.

"Of course," he said as he turned back to Felipe. Illiana would be a beautiful distraction, and he would have to stay focused on his hustle to make sure that things remained professional between them.

Carter sat reserved behind the defense table, completely confident as he sat poised and attentive. It had not been a good day for the defense. After losing their key witness, they were grasping at straws to keep the case alive. Carter's defense was all over it. Beckham was definitely earning his keep as he demolished the federal prosecutor, making Carter look like he was a saint, while discrediting the federal agency that had made his arrest.

"Your Honor, it is clear that without the key witness, the federal prosecutor has no leg to stand on," Beckham stated.

"No, Your Honor, the only thing that is clear is the obvious witness tampering involved in this case. My witness was murdered in cold blood."

"The witness was in protective custody and was rushed to the hospital because of food poisoning," Beckham shot back. "It is on the official State of Pennsylvania police report that the ambulance transporting the witness lost control and crashed. That is how the witness died. My client, who was hundreds of miles away and locked in a prison cell, could not have orchestrated such events!"

"And the bullet holes in his body were just there for decoration!" the D.A. shouted sarcastically. "Your Honor, you can not let this man—this gangster—make a mockery of the law." The prosecutor stood to argue more, but was interrupted by the impatient banging of the judge's gavel.

"Does the State have any other evidence to present besides the witness?" the judge asked.

"No, Your Honor, but—"

"I move for immediate dismissal of the case." Beckham was a shark. He did not even give his adversary a chance to finish his sentence.

All the while, Carter sat back unscathed as he watched the amusing charade go down. It did not matter how much protesting the prosecutor did; he was getting off. The amount of money that the Garza Cartel had put up to make it happen ensured it, and as the judge looked his way, they shared a knowing glance.

"Motion for immediate dismissal granted," the judge announced. The courtroom erupted in mayhem as Carter shook his attorney's hand.

Before Carter could celebrate too much, the prosecutor stood. "Your Honor, the defendant has a new charge pending. He was involved in a prison brawl that resulted in the injury of one of his fellow inmates. We ask that he be held on this new charge that we will be actively pursuing." Carter's eyes burned holes through the white man as the judge approved the request. The government was doing everything in its power to keep him locked up.

Before Carter could even express his displeasure, Beckham leaned into his ear. "Don't worry about it. That is just the desperate measures of a persistent D.A. You just made them look bad. Not many people are able to beat a federal conviction. They are pulling tricks out of their bag to delay your release from prison. I'll make sure that the technicalities are taken care of immediately. You will be out by this evening," Beckham assured.

"Ensure that I am," Carter instructed as he allowed the bailiff to escort him away. He told himself that it was the last time he would ever be placed in handcuffs. Prison was not for him. Although he had gained a valuable new connection behind the wall, he had also had a piece of his soul taken from him, and he would die first before he ever allowed anyone to drag him back to hell.

Mecca sat patiently on Estes' block as he monitored his home. Since he discovered that Leena was alive, she had been on his mind constantly. He was the last person that she wanted to see, but he only needed a moment of her time. She was the only person who could supply him with the answers to the questions he sought.

Her fear of him was evident, and it disturbed Mecca that a woman he had once loved was so terrified of him. Although his anger was still fresh, he had convinced himself that enough was enough. Murder was not the way to solve this problem.

Mecca was tired of killing. He resented his position as the bad seed of his family. Even he had to admit that his aggression and disregard for life had pushed him to the edge. It was one thing to murder because you had to, but Mecca actually enjoyed it. He looked forward to the powerful feeling that taking a life gave him, but it had become a problem when he had begun hurting those that he loved. His ruthless nature was once his best quality when he knew how to control it, but he had taken it too far. Now all he was seeking was redemption.

He had been stalking Estes' house for hours, patiently waiting for his chance to get Leena alone. Finally she emerged, and Mecca admired her closely as she secured his nephew in the backseat of one of Estes' luxury vehicles. He was curious about her relationship with his grandfather, and as she pulled away from the villa, he followed, keeping a comfortable distance so that she would not detect him.

He noticed that Estes had one of his men following Leena as well. It would not be easy for him to get her alone. As she moved in and out of the boutiques on Collins Avenue, Mecca kept a close eye. He was just waiting for the right opportunity to make his move. Estes' men were well trained, and there would be no getting to Leena undetected. The only way for Mecca to approach her would be to go through her protection.

He watched as Leena stopped at a small eatery. He knew that her brief lunch would buy him some time. He parked a block away and then went to the nearest pay phone. He usually hated the police, but today they would aid him in distracting Leena's bodyguard.

He placed a 911 call, giving the police the license plate number to the bodyguard's car, and accusing him of harassing shoppers. Knowing that they were in a prestigious part of town, he knew that the cops would respond almost immediately.

As soon as he saw the squad car flash its lights on the bodyguard, Mecca slipped into the store. Spotting Leena at a quaint table in the back, Mecca approached her.

It was as if her body sensed Mecca's presence. The hairs on the back of her neck stood up and her breath caught in her throat before she even knew he was there. Warning bells went off in her head, and when Leena looked up from her menu, she froze like a deer in headlights. Because of Mecca, she was that tuned in with danger. Mecca's presence made her body tense in trepidation.

"I'm not here to hurt you," Mecca stated peacefully as he stopped where he stood. "I just want to talk to you, that's all."

Leena looked around for her bodyguard, and when she did not see him, she immediately began to gather her things. The small caliber handgun she carried in her child's diaper bag gave her a small peace of mind, but she knew that her shot could not match Mecca's. If he wanted to kill her, he would. She had seen how he got down with her own eyes. She picked up her son. She knew that Mecca would not pop off on her in the crowded eatery. He didn't like witnesses.

As he watched her scramble with her things, his heart broke. At one time, he really had loved her, and he knew that only he was responsible for the fear that she felt toward him.

"Leena, you have my word," Mecca said sincerely. He peered outside of the café window and noticed that the guard was still being harassed by the cop. "Can we go somewhere? Leena, give me at least that."

Leena wanted to tell him no, but she would only be avoiding the inevitable. Mecca was persistent, and his arrogance did not allow for people to turn him down. If she told him no today, he would only come back tomorrow and the day after, until she eventually said yes.

"Lift your shirt," Leena stated, her tone serious.

Mecca lifted his shirt discreetly as he stepped close to Leena, so that the other patrons in the bistro could not see what was going on. She removed his pistol and pressed it against his back. If they were going to talk, it was going to be on her terms. "Walk to the back," she instructed nervously, baby in one hand and gun in the other.

Mecca smiled as Leena took him for a walk out of the back entrance. She had most definitely changed for the better. She was a bit wiser, more cautious, and definitely more street savvy than he remembered. Her time around Estes had not gone by in vain.

When they were finally out in the alley, Leena asked, "What do you want?"

The gun was still pointed in Mecca's back as he replied, "I'm going to turn around now." He chuckled at the irony of the situation and continued. "Whatever you do, don't shoot."

Leena's hand trembled, yet her eyes were determined and revealed to Mecca that she would protect herself if he gave her a reason to. When he was fully facing her, he said, "Is this Money's son?" He already knew the answer to his question, but he needed to hear her confirm it.

He could see a sense of pride and also shame wash over her face as she answered, "Yes."

Mecca smiled at the sight of his nephew. "What happened, Lee?" he asked, calling her by a nickname that only he used. "How did everything get so fucked up?"

Leena steadied her aim as she answered, "I was in love with two brothers. Money and I never meant to hurt you, Mecca."

"He was my brother. How could you fuck with him, Leena? How could he fuck with you? He knew how I felt about you," Mecca whispered.

Leena's eyes widened in disbelief. "How you felt about me, Mecca?" she shrieked. "I didn't even think you were capable of feeling. You wanted Money to see a love that didn't exist."

"You can really stand there and say you didn't love me?" Mecca stated angrily.

"You know I loved you, Mecca . . . but you were the one who never showed it back. Why would Money, or Breeze, or anyone else for that matter know that you loved me? I didn't even know! All you did was ho me, Mecca. You fucked around with this bitch and that bitch, all the while wanting me to stay faithful to you." Utter confusion spread over her face and she stared at him as if everything was his fault.

"Those other bitches didn't mean shit to me, Leena! You knew that! I'm a Diamond."

Leena rolled her eyes at his arrogance and lowered the gun as she dropped it on the ground in disgust, unable to let him finish his sentence. "Yeah, I know you're a Diamond, Mecca. Me and everybody else in Miami knows! That still doesn't give you the right to behave the way you do. It didn't make how you used to treat me hurt any less." She shook her head back and forth. "You know what? I don't even know why we're standing here doing this," she said as she began to turn away. Mecca grabbed her arm to stop her from leaving.

"Leena, I didn't always know how to show it, but I did love you. You were the one I broke bread with. You were the only woman I trusted. You knew everything . . . what I did, where I slept, the combination to the safe. It may have been a fucked up way to love. Shit wasn't sweet or on no lovey-dovey type shit, but it was the only way I knew how to show it," Mecca revealed. "I've never been like Monroe."

"I never asked you to be." Leena stopped him. "But when things got really bad, I began to notice how gentle Monroe was, how patient and loyal he was, and I got caught up. I fell for him. I know that it was wrong, and I knew all along that it would hurt you, but as much as you had hurt me, I did not care. I just wanted to be happy."

"All the bitches in Miami, and Money had to choose mine," Mecca stated callously.

"I think you should know that Money loved you. He loved you so much that he was going to cut everything off with me. The night you caught us, he told me that he would never be with me," Leena admitted.

Hearing this caused Mecca's eyes to become misty as he tried to control his emotions. "I killed him, Lee," Mecca said aloud for the first time as he broke down. There was no reason to lie to her. She had been there. She was the only person in the world who truly knew every aspect of the truth. He hit the concrete wall with his fist.

"You did," Leena replied. Although her heart ached for him, she held back. He did not deserve her sympathy. She could not allow Mecca to pull her back into his chaotic world. Her life was centered, healthy, safe, and nothing but danger dwelled around him.

"I'm sorry, ma. I'm sorry for everything," he finally said, conceding to the guilt that had been torturing him from the very beginning. He did not know what the hell was happening to him, but he did know that the lifestyle he led was slowly becoming harder to maintain. Everything had been so much easier when he had his family behind him. When his father, brother, mother, and sister were alive, he had something to go to war over. He had things to kill for. But now that they all were gone, Mecca felt empty.

"I'm not the person who can forgive you, Mecca. You have

filled your life with so much bad that you have no room left for the good," Leena whispered. "God is the only one who can take the burden away, the guilt. You need to talk to Him."

Mecca nodded his head and gripped the bridge of his nose as he nodded toward his nephew. "Can I hold him?" he asked.

Reluctantly, Leena handed her son to his uncle. The Diamond familial connection was so strong that the little boy instantly took to Mecca. Her eyes filled as she watched her son wrap his arms around Mecca's neck.

"What's good, li'l man?" Mecca greeted as he hugged Monroe Jr. Everything about the little boy reminded him of his late twin. "I owe you the world," he said as he kissed the little boy on the forehead and handed him over to Leena.

Memories of his childhood years with his brother flooded him. It was as if he were staring directly at the past when he looked at Leena's son.

As he began to walk away, one more question nagged at him. He stopped and said, "One more thing. How long have you been living with Estes?"

"Since the day that you shot me," she responded.

Tension filled the space between them as they both recalled that fateful day, and although Mecca had no right to ask, he had to get one more thing off of his chest.

"Are you fucking him?" His tone was not demanding or angry. It was just something he needed to know.

Leena wanted to tell Mecca that it was none of his business, that he was no longer entitled to know who she chose to become intimate with, but she did not. A part of her—the part that felt guilty for sleeping with Monroe, the part that felt guilty for having his brother's child, the part of her that hated the sad look in Mecca's eyes—this part of her allowed her to answer.

"No, Mecca. I'm not sleeping with Estes. He says that he

loves me, but I don't know if I can give it back," Leena replied.

Relief washed over Mecca, and he said, "I want to see you again, and I want to get to know Money's son. I know I have no right to ask, but—"

"Estes will kill you, Mecca. He isn't making idle threats. If he even thinks you are around Money's son . . ." Leena objected. Estes was not her only concern; simply the only one that she voiced.

"I don't care. I have a lot to make up for, Leena. I don't owe Estes shit, but I owe Monroe everything. If you don't want me around, then I'll leave without looking back, but nobody else will stop me from getting to know my brother's son. I'm trying to make things right," he stated sincerely.

"This is all too much for me right now. I love my son, Mecca, and I'm not going to lie; I don't trust you. " Leena opened the back door to the bistro. "I'll think about it. Just give me a little bit of time."

Chapter Ten

"I'm not one of God's children, because I'm too much like the devil."
–Mecca

Carter embraced Garza and patted the old man on the back as they said their final good-byes. It was the inevitable day that they both had orchestrated, and now Carter was leaving with his freedom, while Garza would be left behind.

"Enjoy those cigarettes, old man," Carter joked as he pointed to the boxes that Garza had stacked up in the corner, courtesy of Carter.

"Visit the priest for me. Make sure you give him what he has coming to him, and please ensure that my name is the last one he hears," Garza replied in a low tone.

Carter nodded, letting Garza know that no further words needed to be spoken.

The tier of prisoners erupted in loud, boisterous cheers as Carter made his last walk down their halls. They were giving him praise for beating his case. Carter took it all in stride, never appearing arrogant, and simply making his exit.

Carter emerged from the prison gates with a luxury Lincoln town car awaiting him. Mecca emerged from the back of the car, and the usual tension that dwelled between the half-brothers was non-existent in this moment. Mecca was genuinely happy to see Carter free, because he knew that Carter was the only one who could reorganize The Cartel. Things would be business as usual under Carter's reign.

"Good to see you, boy," Mecca stated.

Carter slapped hands with Mecca and then embraced him tightly. "It's good to see you too, fam. Real good," Carter replied as he stepped inside of the car.

Carter gave the driver Miamor's address. Now that his freedom had been reestablished, hers was the only company he wanted to keep upon his first night home. Her absence from his life had been slowly driving him insane.

He had sent Zyir by her place a few times, only to be told that she never answered the door and was nowhere to be found. He wanted to find out for himself, because he knew Miamor well. It was not in her character to leave him on stuck when he needed her most.

With the Garza Cartel connection being secured by Zyir, he knew that all of the pieces of his life were about to realign. She was the only thing missing. The center of his puzzle was lost and he had to find it, because without her, everything would be for nothing.

Mecca rode silently as he looked out of the window. *The sooner this ol' lovesick nigga get over this bitch, the easier it's gon' be on him. Ain't no coming back from the place I sent her*, he thought. A part of him just wanted to tell Carter the truth, but he knew that it would only complicate things. So, he allowed Carter to go on the dummy mission of searching for a girl he would never find.

"I had Zyir looking for Miamor while I was locked up. He said you told him she had skipped town," Carter said as they pulled up to Miamor's high-rise building.

"That's what I heard. The bitch is bad news, bro. The way you were wife'n her before you went in, she should have been the one by your side through it all. She didn't stand tall, my nigga. Before the ink on the indictment papers dried, she got ghost on you. Fuck her, fam. It ain't worth the headache. You're out, and it's time to move forward."

Mecca's advice would have resounded loud and clear if had been any other woman besides Miamor, but she was like an infection of the heart. Letting go would not be so easy.

Knowing that Mecca was too callous to understand the connection he shared with Miamor, he changed the subject. "When Zyir arrives, it's back to business. Until then, I'm going to lay low and get my mind right. I have a couple of loose ends to clip before the shipment arrives," he said.

Mecca nodded. "Your car will be delivered tomorrow morning."

Carter exited the car and made his way up to Miamor's condo. Although he had a key to her place, he knocked politely, not wanting to intrude. When he didn't get an answer, he opened the door anyway and stepped inside. He immediately knew that she had not been there lately. The smell of rotting food permeated through the condo, and she had twenty new messages on her answering machine. As he moved through the apartment, his suspicions arose.

Where are you, ma? he asked as he inventoried her bedroom. Her closets and dressers were still filled with clothes. He knew that she didn't leave town, because she would never leave her possessions behind. As he collapsed onto her bed, his gut twisted in premonition. He had a feeling that her disappearance was not coincidental, and he was determined to find out exactly where she had gone.

But first, he had a message to deliver. Josiah Garza was about to reach out from behind the prison walls and seek vengeance for an unspeakable crime committed against him many years ago.

***

Leena's words haunted Mecca: *God is the only one who can take the burden away, the guilt. You need to talk to Him.*

He knew that she was right. He had never been a religious man, but the crimes that he had committed against his own family were torturing him. *If there really is a God, I need Him to take the pain away,* Mecca thought.

Although he had no regrets about killing Miamor, he did hate himself because he knew that by doing so, he had taken away someone who had meant the world to his brother. Carter was all he had left, and he feared that if the truth were ever revealed, he would have no one. For the first time in his life, Mecca felt remorse for things that he had done that hurt other people.

Even he had to admit that if he had not murdered Miamor's sister, then she would have never come after his family. He had lived his life recklessly, without regard for others. Any way he tried to spin the situation, everything, all of the chaos and misery, led back to him. He had been the spark of it all. Mecca was the root of all evil. Bullets had been the answer to all of his problems, and now all of the lives he had taken were coming back to haunt him. He could barely sleep at night because he was afraid to close his eyes. If he could make amends, he would, but there was no reversing the things he had done.

As he sat in front of the Catholic Church, he knew that there was only one thing left to do: give his burdens to God and hope that his soul was capable of being cleansed. He wasn't a Catholic, but knew that he could never confess his wrongdoings to a black minister. His business would travel through Miami's gossip grapevine for sure. So, he chose a place where he could be low key. Confessing to a white man in a white church, he was confident that the conversation would go no further than the four walls of the cathedral.

As he stepped out of the car, he felt his gun on his hip. As many people as he had murdered, it would be foolish to leave it behind. But he removed it from his waistline anyway and placed it beneath his car seat. Despite the fact that his conscience screamed for him to stay strapped, he did not want to carry the weapon inside of the church. He took a deep breath as he headed for the entrance, feeling as though his judgment day had arrived.

Carter walked side by side with the priest of St. Jude Catholic Church as he explained the concept of forgiveness and redemption. Carter had spent the past hour speaking with the old man at the request of Garza. Garza wanted to know if the priest displayed any remorse for the children he had betrayed in his past, and Carter followed his directions precisely. He was given specific instructions: "If the priest shows remorse, kill him quickly. If not, then a slow death will be better suited," Garza had said.

"Have you ever done something that you are not proud of, Father?" Carter asked as they sat down near the front of the church.

"Son, no man is without sin. There are things that I have done in my past that God will hold me accountable for," the priest replied as he became slightly emotional. "Some things that I have done I can never take back."

"Father, I'm here to hold you accountable for those actions," Carter stated in a low, serious tone. "Josiah Garza sent me."

The old white man's eyes widened in paralyzing fear as he allowed the emotion in his eyes to fall down his wrinkled cheeks. He knew exactly who Carter spoke of, and his mind flashed back to the acts of molestation he had committed against Garza when he was only a small boy. It was then that he realized that today would be his last day on this earth. The priest began to weep as he leaned forward, resting his head on Carter's shoulder.

Carter didn't speak as he closed his eyes. He removed his .38 pistol from the jacket of his Brooks Brothers suit and placed the barrel directly against the priest's chest. He allowed the old man to weep on his shoulder as he pulled the trigger, sending a bullet piercing through his heart.

"Forgive me, Father," Carter whispered.

Even the dull sound of the silenced bullet echoed slightly against the walls of the cathedral. Carter caught the old man's body as gravity took it to the floor, and he laid him down to rest behind one of the church pews. The old man's eyes stared up into space, and Carter closed them. It wasn't a task that Carter had wanted to do, but he had given his word. The old man had it coming to him for all of the abuse he had inflicted on the young boys of his parish over the years.

The clanking sound of the doors opening startled Carter.

"Fuck," he whispered, knowing that he could never make it to the back door without being seen. He made sure that the priest's body was out of sight, and then slid into the confessional. He hoped that the intruder would come and go quickly, without throwing a wrench in his program. He had planned to execute the priest quietly, without interruption. Carter did not want to have to hurt an innocent bystander for being in the wrong place at the wrong time. The tension in his body was so high that he could hear his own heartbeat.

The other side of the confessional opened and Carter prepared himself to take another life. He saw the shadow of a man sit across from him on the other side of the lattice. Carter pointed the gun to the center of the shadow's face, but the voice that he heard come from the other side stopped him from shooting. He froze as he listened to a confession that he was never meant to hear.

"Forgive me, Father, for I have sinned," Mecca stated. "I don't know how this usually works, but I'm just gonna speak my piece. I feel like this is the only place where I can admit the truth without being judged. I know I'm not a good man. I've known it all along . . . ever since I was a kid. There was always something evil living inside of me, but I kept it dormant for a long time, until the day I killed my twin brother. I have a lot of blood on my hands, Father, but the blood of my brother I can't seem to wash away. It's like I see it on my hands all day." Mecca lowered his head into his hands. Even admitting his sins behind the protection of anonymity was hard.

"I murdered my brother out of rage, out of jealousy, and then I lied to my entire family to cover my tracks. It feels like I've been lying ever since. I murdered my older brother's girlfriend, and I look him in the face every day, watching the hurt in his eyes. I pretend like I don't know why it's there, when in actuality I caused it. When he asks about her, I plant seeds in his head to make him think she left town, when I know I left her in a basement in pieces.

"The sick part about it is that I enjoyed it. I know only God has the power to judge, but I was that bitch's judge, jury, and executioner. She took too much away from me to let her live.

"My father would be ashamed of me. He put family above all else, and all of his sons were built just like him—except for me. Money was a good nigga, Father." Mecca choked up and stopped speaking momentarily to get himself together. "He was my other half.

"My older brother is so much like our pops that it scares

me. I know I'm not one of God's children, because I'm too
much like the devil, but I'm tired, Father. I just want the de-
mons in me to die. I want to be like my father—good."

Carter sat on the other side of the booth with his finger wrapped tightly around the trigger of his pistol. Disbelief
clouded his brain as he pictured Miamor's face in his head.
He pointed the gun directly at Mecca's face. All he had to do
was let off one shot to make things right. With one bullet,
the deaths of Miamor and Monroe could be avenged, but the
fact that Mecca was his brother made him hesitate. They both
came from the same bloodline. They were the last of a dying
breed. Carter wasn't sure if he would be able to live with his
decision if he chose to kill Mecca.

Carter put his hands to his face as he felt the hot tears
threaten to fall. He was in utter turmoil just at the thought
of Miamor's death. She had been his life, his everything, the
woman that he had wanted to marry. He had planned to
spend an eternity with her, and in the blink of an eye, she had
been taken away. Mecca had robbed him of his only chance in
life to be truly happy. Miamor was his happiness.

Carter already knew of the basement that Mecca spoke of.
It was The Cartel's torture chamber, and he knew that Mecca
had made her suffer a horrible death. He could hear Mecca
crying as he poured out his sins, and Carter closed his eyes,
allowing his own silent tears to fall. Both brothers sat on differences sides of the booth in turmoil.

The nigga deserve to die. All of this, this entire war started be-
cause of the lies he told. Everybody would still be alive if it wasn't
for Mecca. We broke the truce with the Haitians because we thought
they were responsible for Money. All along it's been him, Carter
thought. His rage was so prevalent that it burned his insides,

making him feel as though he would explode at any moment. Hearing Mecca's confession and finally finding out the truth caused his stomach to turn violently. He was sick with grief. He had loved Mecca and trusted him.

How could he kill Money? He was our brother, Carter thought. *How did I miss what was right in front of my face for so long? Mecca murdered Miamor.*

Carter couldn't grasp the fact that two people he had cared dearly for had been ripped from underneath him. It was unfathomable, and even though he had heard the words come directly from Mecca's mouth, he still did not want to believe them. Carter remembered all of the lies that Mecca had told to cover his tracks as he watched Mecca rise and begin to walk away. It was up to him to end Mecca's reign of terror, but he could not do it. Sitting underneath's God's watchful eye, all he could do was mourn the deaths of those he had lost at the hands of his only remaining sibling.

When Mecca exited the church, Carter stood to his feet and stumbled out of the confession booth. He stepped over the priest's dead body and down the long aisle of the church. He palmed his gun tightly in his hand; the security of having it locked and loaded reassured him. He had no idea what his next move would be, but there was one thing that he was sure of: his brother, Mecca, could not be trusted.

The nigga has destroyed everything around him. It'll only be a matter of time before he comes for me.

"What's the matter, Zyir? You're not used to riding in things this big?" Illiana asked as she lit a cigarette and blew the smoke into the air. "You're going fifty-five miles per hour. The limit is seventy."

Zyir sighed as he reached over and pulled the cigarette from between her lips. She had been talking nonstop since they left Mexico, and he was more than tired of hearing her talk slick out of the side of her neck.

"Hey!" she objected as she turned in her seat and looked at Zyir in irritation.

"I said no cigarettes," Zyir replied as he kept his eyes fixed on the road in front of him. Driving from Mexico back to Miami was a four-day trip, and he was sure to go crazy with Illiana riding shotgun.

Illiana rolled her eyes and crossed her hands over her chest. She pointed at the highway sign and said, "Pull over at the next stop."

"What the fuck for?" Zyir asked. "I can't keep stopping every hour. We'll never make it back at this rate."

"I have to piss, so unless you want me to soak these fucking seats, pull over at the next stop," Illiana replied bossily.

Zyir glared over at her. He had to bite his tongue to stop himself from barking on her. It was obvious that she was used to men catering to her every whim. *This bitch is going to drive me crazy*, Zyir thought as he pulled over at the next rest stop. "Hurry up," he instructed.

Illiana purposefully took her time as she watched Zyir through the window of the truck stop. She enjoyed giving him a hard time. It was foreplay for her. Since the moment she had seen him, he held her attention. He was focused, powerful, and had a dominant personality that piqued her interest. It was she who had convinced Felipe to send her to Miami. It would be the perfect opportunity for her to get to know Zyir. She was a woman who did not understand the word *no*, and when she saw something she wanted, she went after it relentlessly. Zyir was in her line of sight and he did not even know it.

As she finally emerged from the rest stop, she noticed Zyir

standing outside of the truck, waiting impatiently and looking around cautiously.

"Relax. Nobody's watching, Zyir. You American boys are so paranoid. You watch too many gangster movies. My brother has moved shipments like this for years and nothing has ever gone wrong," she stated as she stood directly in front of him. She was standing so closely that she could feel the imprint of his penis rubbing against her. The thin linen fabric of her sundress blew in the wind, and she made no effort to move.

Zyir smirked at her blatant attempts at flirtation. "Get in the car. We're not stopping again," Zyir stated in a firm tone as he pushed her gently away from him and hopped back into the truck.

Zyir got back onto the Interstate as Illiana reached for the radio to turn it up. Zyir immediately switched it back off.

"What, the radio isn't allowed either?" Illiana asked. "I'm supposed to ride for days without any entertainment?"

"I can't hear the sirens if the radio is blasting," Zyir answered simply. "Read one of your magazines or something."

"I guess I'll have to entertain myself then," she replied with a mischievous smile as she opened her legs and slipped her fingers up her dress. She played with her clit as one of her straps fell off her shoulder. Zyir peered over and almost slid off the road as he swerved in surprise.

"What are you doing?" he asked as he cleared his throat uncomfortably and regained control of the wheel.

"You told me to read or something. This is something," she whispered. The look in her eyes radiated lust as she put on a one-woman show for Zyir.

He couldn't help but to look over at the lovely sight as she closed her eyes and worked her fingers in and out of her wetness. He could see her juices flowing onto the seat.

"You can touch it, Zyir. I know you want to." Everything about Illiana was inviting; even her words teased his ears as he struggled to keep his attention focused on the road. His manhood hardened at the visual Illiana was providing him with.

Illiana was a seductress, and she laughed slightly because she knew that Zyir was trying to resist the inevitable. She crawled across the front seat of the cabin and climbed into Zyir's lap, straddling him.

"Yo, fuck is you doing, ma?" Zyir asked, his voice low with indecision as he continued to drive. "You gon' make me crash this big mu'fucka."

Illiana reached down and massaged his hard-on through his cargo shorts before removing it from its confinements. "Hmm," she moaned as she kissed his neck.

The scent of her invaded his nostrils as he gave in to the temptation. She was too beautiful to resist, too enticing to turn away, and although he knew that mixing business with pleasure was for the foolish, Illiana was too hard to turn away. Just like all of the other men she had encountered, he could not tell her no.

"Let me pull over," Zyir whispered as his breath caught in his throat when she slid down on his shaft. She was so tight that it felt as if his dick was in a glove specifically sized for him. "Damn, ma."

"No, keep driving. Don't stop," Illiana moaned as she worked her hips in circles, enjoying how he filled her up perfectly, taking up all the space in her pussy. The girth of him took her breath away as she rode him slowly.

The ecstasy was so great that Zyir could not stop his eyes from closing. He was high off of the feeling that Illiana was giving him, and the harder she rode down on him, the faster he pushed the large Mack truck. The mixture of speed and sex tickled his loins as his adrenaline rushed him. He removed one hand from the steering wheel to grip her voluptuous behind.

"Ooh, Zy, cum with me, papi," she urged as she felt the intensity building between her thighs. The sound of her voice in his ear as she rode him only heightened his lust for her. Zyir was ready to pull over and beat it up.

"Ride it faster, ma," he coached.

Illiana began to work her vaginal muscles, tensing them around his thickness until Zyir could no longer take it. He lifted her off of him with one hand just as he exploded. He closed his eyes, and his mouth fell open as he rode the power-ful wave of the orgasm.

"Zyir!" Illiana yelled as the truck veered into the next lane. She grabbed the steering wheel, laughing hysterically, until Zyir regained his composure.

"Is it too much to ask for you to pull over again at the next stop so I can clean up?" she asked.

Zyir nodded and gave her a rare smile, turning his usual serious face into the most handsome one she had ever seen

"Yeah, ma. Whatever you want. I got you," he replied.

Carter stood outside of the house where Mecca had mur-dered Miamor. It wasn't hard to find. The Cartel had used the dilapidated structure many times before. Things didn't make sense to him. He did not understand why Mecca had taken such extreme measures.

What did she do to deserve this? he thought as he stepped foot inside. The stench of death invaded his nose instantly. It was almost too much for him to stomach.

Making his way down the basement steps, he saw the rem-nants of Miamor's murder. The floor was painted with stains of her blood, and the entire room only gave him unwanted images of her death. He stood in the middle of the room as he absorbed it all. He could feel Miamor's ghost lingering over him. It pained him, because he would never even get to lay her to rest properly.

"I'm sorry," he whispered aloud as he turned to leave. As he looked back one last time, he noticed something on the floor. A necklace, one identical to the one that he wore, lay near the wooden chair. He walked over to it and picked up. His hands instinctively went to his own neck to touch the small cross that hung from it. It had been a gift from their father, and because they were the only two left, he knew that it was Mecca's.

The walls of the basement began to close in on him as his grief threatened to swallow him whole. Not only had he lost his woman, but his brother as well. No matter how he chose to resolve the situation, things would never be the same. With a new connect, things were supposed to be looking up, but deceit was threatening to tear The Cartel apart from the inside out.

His cell phone rang just as he made his exit. He answered it immediately, already knowing that it was Zyir.

"Zy, I got to talk to you about Mecca."

"I just got off the phone with him. We about to get this money, fam. Mecca's on his way to the warehouse. Meet me there."

"I'm on my way, but do me a favor, Zyir. Don't trust Mecca. Be careful around him. I'll explain later," Carter replied in a tone of warning.

"No explanation needed. It wasn't a day that I didn't move carefully around him anyway, fam. A nigga with a body count like that you gotta watch, nah mean?"

Carter walked into the warehouse to the most beautiful sight he had ever seen. Three thousand kilos of cocaine sat lined neatly side by side, one on top of the other, composing a wall of riches before him. The math was easy to do. Flipping that many birds meant that they were about to be stupid rich.

"Yeah, boy, you can crack a smile. No need to be the boss at all times," Zyir joked as he slapped hands with Carter and embraced him briefly. He missed Mecca with the introductions. He had no desire to show his brother love when all he was feeling in his heart was hate.

"We're back. I can put this work out a.s.a.p. Let niggas know the drought is over," Mecca stated.

Carter stared at Mecca for a long time and found it hard to conceal his rage. Fire burned in his eyes, and even the stature of his presence was stiff, cold, as if Mecca were the enemy.

"What's good, Carter? You a'ight?" Mecca asked. He had no idea that his secret was out, but as he looked in his older sibling's eyes, he felt that the times of treachery were headed his way.

"Everything's good. Just thinking about how niggas might want to steer clear of stepping on my toes. I made the mistake of trusting Ace too much. It's always the closest niggas to you that do the most harm," Carter replied while never averting Mecca's gaze.

"Nah, baby, you don't put in work. You just sit back and drive this ship. Take us to the money like only you can do. Me and Zy can handle the beef. All snake-ass niggas have been taken care of," Mecca replied.

"It's always one left hiding in the grass," Carter responded.

The tension in the room was high and put Mecca slightly on edge. He felt as if he were staring into the eyes of his father. It felt like Carter was looking straight through him, and the only other man who had ever been able to make him feel so transparent was their father.

Zyir was silent because he knew Carter well. He was speaking in codes, and Mecca didn't even have a clue that the beef Carter had was with him.

Larcenous-ass nigga, Carter thought.

Zyir pulled two keys from his pocket and handed one to both men. "I had the locks changed. Only the three of us have access to this building, so each and every bird should always be accounted for," Zyir stated. "Felipe sent his sister Illiana back to Miami with me. She's here to protect their investment . . . a set of eyes for the Garza Cartel."

"Where is she now?" Carter asked.

"I took her to my crib. I didn't know if you wanted her to know the location of the warehouse. Three thousand joints are too many to take any risks," Zyir stated.

"You can show her, and only her, where we keep 'em," Carter stated. "She doesn't need a key, however. If the Mexicans want her here to make sure everything is moving right, then we have nothing to hide from them. It'll show good faith."

Carter began to walk away, and Zyir stated, "I know we gon' celebrate tonight. This is a power move we're making."

Carter turned around and shook his head as he looked at Mecca. Disappointment, anger, sadness . . . it all consumed him simultaneously. Without responding, Carter made his exit. He had thought when he emerged from prison that all of his problems would be behind him, but now the dilemmas in his life seemed even more prevalent than before.

"Fuck is up with him?" Mecca stated.

Zyir feigned ignorance and replied, "I don't know, but I'd hate to be a problem of his. Just because he don't talk about it, don't mean he ain't about it, nah mean? Carter ain't about playing gangster. He don't got to be all extra in order to get his point across. That macho shit is for dumb niggas, and dumb mu'fuckas are the easiest to clip."

***

Zyir sat in the apartment like a seasoned chemist as he took it back to his humble roots, cooking dope with ten naked women around him. The titties and ass that were on display were of no interest to him. It only ensured that nobody got sticky fingers. Theft was impossible when you wore no clothes to stash the product. The Cartel took to the streets like never before, and in addition to selling the bricks wholesale, they had chosen to break down three hundred of them.

Zyir was a perfectionist when it came to stretching cocaine, and he was more than willing to put in the work to turn three hundred into six hundred, with the help of the lovely ladies around him. While Mecca thought he was above serving fiends, Zyir wasn't for turning away a single dollar. He loved money, and while Mecca had the wholesale market covered, Zyir was taking over the streets. He kept it hood and set up his operation on every inner city block in Dade County.

He wasn't about the gunplay, because he did not need any unnecessary attention from the boys in blue, so instead of forcing his competition out, he played fair and simply offered them an opportunity to work for him. His affiliation with The Cartel put stars in niggas' eyes and they instantly jumped at the chance just to be down by association. Zyir had so many hustlers working for him that he never personally saw the blocks. He simply organized the operation, supplied the dope, and sat back as the money piled in. Nobody caused conflicts because everybody was eating.

Miami had never seen a movement like The Cartel's. It was calculated carefully and executed with efficiency. It was all about the money, and the more they accumulated, the more the streets began to forget the troubles that had plagued them surrounding the law.

The Cartel was back and better than ever. They had learned from their mistakes, and this time what they were building was untouchable. The only thing that could tear down their empire was self-destruction.

Chapter Eleven

"Young Zyir is simply a protégé of yours. You both are men
of little patience, always eager to get to the dinero."
—*Felipe*

Carter pulled up to Felipe's estate. He had moved through
the bricks and it was re-up time. Carter made hustling look
easy. Most men wouldn't know how to handle one brick, and
within a month, he had burned through three thousand. Now
he was back in Mexico to pay the piper.

He was eager to meet his connect face to face for the first
time. He no longer needed Zyir to play middleman. Now that
he was free, he could handle his own affairs.

He was unimpressed by the opulence around him as he
entered Felipe Garza's estate. If anything, the flashiness of the
place turned him off. It was obvious that Felipe was living the
lavish life, and Carter only hoped that his new connect was
smart enough to ensure his longevity. If Felipe's spotlight was
too bright, then others would surely be watching. The estate
was beautiful, but it was excessive and massive, too much for
any one man.

Carter hoped that linking up with this new connect did
not prove to be a costly mistake. He took a deep breath to
calm himself before he exited the car. His recent stay in prison had caused him to be increasingly aware of every move he
made. He viewed the streets as a chess game, and he wanted
nothing more than to win.

"Carter Jones, my brother Josiah Garza speaks highly of you. It is good to finally meet with you," Felipe greeted, extending his hand as the two men shook.

"Likewise. I know this visit is unexpected. We were not scheduled to meet for another three months, but I like to move quickly . . . efficiently," Carter stated.

"I understand. I was under the impression that we would meet once you were done with the entire package. It does me no good to receive my money in pieces. I'd like the entire forty million back at one time," Felipe replied.

Before he responded, he walked over to the limo and knocked on the window. The driver emerged and popped the trunk where duffel bag after duffel bag filled the interior.

"Like I said, I move quickly. That's the entire forty with an extra five for you as repayment for the work you put in concerning my case," Carter stated. "You can have your men unload it. The first deal proved to be very lucrative. Let us waste no time in doing it again."

Although it was Carter who was the guest, he took charge as if he were on home turf. He held out his arm and motioned for Felipe to walk with him. He could see the displeasure in Felipe's eyes. The Mexican drug lord was used to other men following his lead, but it was clear that Carter Jones had no intentions of playing the back. He was a boss, and conducted himself as such.

Felipe had taken a keen interest in Zyir. He had liked the young fellow because he had displayed the proper etiquette in dealing with someone superior to him. Carter, however, had put a different taste in his mouth. In his presence, Felipe felt inadequate, and it was then that he realized that all of the things he had heard about The Cartel was true. He was staring into the eyes of their leader, a man even greater than himself. Carter had experienced a minor setback when he had fallen under a federal microscope, but now that things were back on track, he had the potential to overthrow any empire. Felipe knew that this was not the intention of Carter, but his demeanor indicated that it was always a possibility. Felipe would have to be careful with how much power he helped The Cartel re-attain.

"Now I see that young Zyir is simply a protégé of yours. You both are men of little patience, always eager to get to the dinero," Felipe stated. "Let us get to know each other as men first, and then we will discuss our arrangement. I own a few brothels and gentlemen's establishments that I'm sure you will enjoy."

Carter nodded and obliged with a discreet smirk because he knew that Felipe was trying to feel him out. He had sent Zyir to Mexico with specific instructions to go with the flow, because he did not know what he was getting his li'l man into. He, on the other hand, was there to establish boundaries and to ensure that both parties understood each other clearly. He wasn't there to party and bullshit, but this would give him a perfect opportunity to turn the tables and learn more about the Garza Cartel's operation.

Murder discreetly picked the lock to Miamor's old condo, the same place where Carter had recently taken residence, and slipped inside. The place still held Miamor's scent, and Carter had removed none of her old belongings, which made memories of his li'l mama come rushing back to Murder. It was as if she still lived there and could walk through the door at any moment.

Being so close to The Cartel was eating him alive. He was in the same city and had barely made a move on them yet. He didn't want to make the same mistakes that had cost Miamor her life. He wanted to study them from afar first, before moving in. Without a doubt, he knew that Mecca had been the one to end Miamor's life, but that did not relieve the blame from Carter's shoulders so easily. He wanted revenge on them all. Carter was the leader, and above all else, he had chosen to wife Miamor. He should have ensured her protection.

What type of nigga lets his chick be murdered in cold blood? Murder thought.

Murder would have never let anything happen to Miamor. She had been the only woman he had ever loved. He remembered how infectious her personality was, how easy it was to become consumed in her beauty, how he would have done anything for her. He concluded that any man who truly loved Miamor could have never let this happen.

Miamor was the type of woman that you kept shielded from the world because she could not be replaced. She had been a rare find, an unspoiled soul with a ruthless talent for killing. There was not another soul like hers in existence, and now that she was gone, Murder saw nothing but black. There was no white in his world, no silver lining around his dark cloud. She had been the best part of him, and even from afar and through the isolation of the prison walls, he had loved her. She wasn't simply the type of chick who would blow through your money and whisper sweet nothings in your ear. She was the type to blow a hole through a nigga and hit his safe right next to her man if need be. She was loyal.

Before Murder had ever gotten a chance to truly build a life with her, Carter had come along, snatching her heart from underneath him.

Murder moved quickly through the condominium. He wasn't exactly sure what he was looking for. He simply needed to know more, and with Carter out of town on business, this was the perfect opportunity for him to search for answers.

He came across a photo of Miamor and Carter. The happy snapshot featured the couple vacationing on a beach. Jealousy burned through him as he placed the picture face down on the mantle.

Just as he was about to make his exit, he noticed a book that stuck out slightly from the collection on the bookshelf. He walked over to it and pulled it gently. As he suspected, a trap door opened, and Murder slipped inside. It looked like an army's arsenal closet. For a man of Murder's profession, it was like being a kid in a candy store as he admired all of the flawless guns. He knew the room had not been meant for anyone's eyes but Miamor's. It was where she kept all of the details of the jobs she accepted, and tacked to the wall was a huge picture of Mecca Diamond with a red circle around it.

As he stared at the extensive research that Miamor had done on the Diamond family, he was amazed. She had been so detailed, so precise. She had indeed become the best at what she did. Even Murder did not realize what she was capable of. She even had monitors that showed the inside of her own home, so that when she was inside of the room, she would know exactly who was inside her place and what room they were located in.

He froze when he heard the lock to the front door turn. Luckily, Murder had made his way through the condo in the dark, and his identity was hidden behind the ski mask he wore. He turned off his flashlight and pulled the trap door closed as he watched the monitor to see who was coming inside. His temple throbbed when he saw Mecca Diamond enter.

Mecca had noticed that Carter had been throwing him shade lately, and he had a feeling that it had something to do with Miamor. He wanted to know how much Carter actually knew. It would give him a better idea of how to play the situation. He left the lights off as he moved through the place.

As Murder watched Mecca disappear through the monitors, he crept out quietly, .45 in his hand. Killing Mecca would be sweet for him, and as he stood in the middle of the living room, he contemplated his options. The Murder Mamas had advised him to play his cards right. If he hit Mecca tonight, it would throw a red flag to the rest of the members of The Cartel. There would be a contract out for Mecca's murderer almost immediately, and with everybody on edge, it would make it even harder for Murder to get to Carter.

He silently headed for the door and was about to leave when an overwhelming hatred for Mecca overcame him. His murder game clicked on, and he turned on his heel and headed toward the bedroom.

Fuck hitting these niggas all at once. Another opportunity like this ain't gonna present itself, Murder thought as he preyed on Mecca, letting his gun lead the way down the pitch black hallway.

Mecca used the tiny flashlight as his only illumination as he went through Carter's possessions. When he found the small 14 karat gold cross that his father had given him, he froze. He hadn't seen it since the day he killed Miamor. He had beaten her so mercilessly that it had fallen from his neck. The fact that Carter now had it meant that Carter had been to Mecca's torture house. He had seen the tools that had been used to torture Miamor.

He knows, Mecca thought. He had hoped that it would not have to come to this. He had witnessed firsthand how much Carter cared for Miamor, and this would surely put them at odds.

He just couldn't let the bitch go. That's why he's been looking at me sideways. Fuck! Mecca thought. He knew what had to be done, but was no longer sure if he could do it. He did not want to murder another brother. He was trying to become a better man, and it was no longer in him to take the life of someone he loved.

As Mecca thought over his dilemma, an eerie feeling suddenly came over him. He was a breed of mankind that had not been reproduced yet, and he instantly knew that someone was behind him. He could almost smell the gunpowder from the weapon that was pointed at the back of his head.

Mecca bucked back violently. "Aghh!" He screamed as he pushed back with all his might, throwing Murder off balance as Mecca rammed him into the wall.

A fight between the two men was useless. They were both too skilled to get the best of the other. Every blow Mecca threw, Murder blocked, and each time Murder wrapped his finger around the trigger, Mecca averted his aim. Their battle was like a synchronized dance as they attacked each other with full force, each becoming increasingly frustrated because neither could gain the upper hand.

"Who the fuck sent you?" Mecca barked. He was not sure who was gunning for him now. It could easily be Estes, but with this new revelation, it could be Carter as well.

Murder finally managed to get his finger around the trigger, and he fired relentlessly as he wrestled with Mecca for control of the gun. Sparks erupted from the barrel of the gun like a fireworks display on the Fourth of July.

Murder's skinny build failed him in a fistfight. He would shoot the shit out of a nigga before he ever sparred with him, but Mecca, on the other hand, was good with his hands. Mecca's well-built, solid frame allowed him to finally overpower Murder, causing the gun to go flying across the room.

Murder knew that Mecca was strapped, and went for the only exit in the room, the bedroom balcony. He ran full force, breaking through the glass, and disappeared before Mecca could get off a shot. Mecca was far from a rookie, however. It was the same exact escape that he had used to get away from Estes' goons, and his hollow point bullets could swim. He knew to aim straight for the pool below.

He reached out and rushed to lean over the balcony, only to find the pool undisturbed below.

"Fucking nigga ain't Superman. Where the fuck did he—" Mecca stated in confusion, but before he could even finish his sentence, Murder's gun emerged from the balcony below. Without hesitation, he fired, hitting Mecca in the face.

Murder was grateful that he always carried a weapon on his ankle as he ran through the empty condo and out the front door, where he skirted off into the night.

The music in the club blared loudly as Carter sat back in the booth while a beautiful Mexican girl danced in front of him. His eyes graced the delicate curves of her body as she put on the best performance he had ever seen. Seeing her before him made him feel empty inside. Outwardly, no one would be able to tell that he was in turmoil, but in the privacy of his heart, he was broken from losing Miamor.

I should have been there for her. I could have stopped Mecca if she had just come to me. How did I not know what was going on right underneath my nose? A part of Carter felt like he did not even know Miamor. She had lived a lifestyle so closely linked to his that it was scary. His logic told him that he had been a target of hers along with the rest of The Cartel, but he could never bring himself to believe that she would ever bring him harm. The love that they had built was too deep, and although so many things she had told him had been lies, he knew that her feelings for him had been truth. He was in a daze as he thought of her, placing her face on the dancer in front of him.

"They don't make tits like these in Miami, eh?" Felipe asked, interrupting Carter's thoughts. "This is pure bred Mexicana pussy," he bragged as he tipped generously and sipped at his glass of cognac.

Carter chuckled as he raised his glass to acknowledge the beauty that surrounded him in the club.

"This is the business that you need to get into. The drug money is good, but this is where it's at," Felipe stated surely.

"Prostitution?" Carter said doubtfully.

Felipe shook his head and smiled coyly while pointing at Carter. "No, my friend. That's where you're wrong." He pointed to the girls around the club. "This right here, this is just one entity. Trafficking, that's what I'm into. I buy and sell girls. I put them to work in clubs, brothels, on the street. Sex is man's biggest addiction, Carter. I supply that demand, and it makes me filthy rich. Let me show you something."

Carter stood and followed Felipe through the club as he explained his operation. "This club is one of many of my establishments. I own every property on this street, and each one serves its purpose." Felipe led Carter out the front door and then pointed to the house next door. "That house right there is the brothel, and the one next to it is an auction house."

"An auction house, as in slave auctions," Carter stated condescendingly.

"Modern day slavery, if that is what you would like to call it. Human trafficking is big business. It is happening all over the world. I buy my girls from all over and I put them to work. Pump 'em up on heroin and they'll do anything I say."

"How do you keep them from running away?" Carter asked as they stepped into the brothel house.

"Where are they going to go? They have no one, no family. They come from many different places. Some from Africa, some from Asia, the Caribbean . . . you name it. All they have is me and the addiction that holds them hostage," Felipe replied.

The house was littered with drug paraphernalia. Dirty needles lay out on tables, and the smell of sex filled the air. Carter was almost too disgusted to continue the tour. He could only imagine the type of clientele that frequented the spot. Brothel was just a friendly name for a whorehouse, in his opinion, and he knew that this would never be a type of venture he would be interested in taking. He didn't believe in exploitation, and as Carter looked around the house he knew that the women trapped there were simply waiting to die.

"The money never touches the girls' hands. The men pay the madame on the way in," Felipe stated.

He expected Carter to be impressed, but his creased brow revealed his contempt. His moral compass allowed him to do many things. He had killed, robbed, and deceived, but to kill a person's soul and force them into prostitution was beyond Carter's ability. His moral compass would not allow him to ever become that lost.

"I know what you're thinking. You think I'm running a trashy establishment here," Felipe stated. "I only buy the best girls. Let me show you the grade-A pussy I'm selling here."

He led Carter up the stairs to one of the closed bedroom doors. Before Felipe opened it, he said, "All you need is a few like this one in here, and men will come from everywhere to sample her. She is my big moneymaker."

He opened the door, and when Carter stepped in, his heart broke in half. The sight before him almost brought him to his knees. It was as if he were seeing a ghost.

She's supposed to be dead. How long has she been here?

As the girl lifted her head, her eyes met Carter's. It had been a long time since they had seen one another. It was a reunion that neither of them ever thought would come. Before him was Breeze Diamond, on her knees in front of a john. She was so high out of her mind that she did not believe what was appearing before her very eyes. She had imagined her family too many times to get her hopes up. She was so high that she thought Carter was simply another customer waiting to be serviced. She shed a single tear as she lowered her head back into the man's crotch and went back to work.

Zyir sat back on his plush king-sized bed as he and Illiana counted the money he had just collected from the streets. The first flip had been good, and everybody was eating again. In fact, the streets had never seen a cocaine epidemic like the one that The Cartel was pushing. It was a new day, and although internal tensions were at an all-time high, everybody was putting their differences aside, because they all saw the bigger picture. It was time to move on and let past beefs die. The Cartel was in a stage of rebuilding, and money was always the common denominator that put everyone on the same page.

"How much is that?" he asked as he threw a large stack at Illiana, causing her to drop the blunt that was hanging loosely from her lips. It fell onto the exposed skin of her thigh.

"Damn it, Zy!" she screamed as she frantically hopped up, wearing nothing but lace panties and one of his button-up shirts. "You burnt the shit out of me," she whined.

"You'll be a'ight. Finish counting that," Zyir instructed. He continued the count in his head as he began to flip through a new stack of money. He was a mathematician when it came to his paper. The sound of the bills flipping through the money machine was like a classic melody to him, but even he questioned its accuracy. After the machine counted it, he counted it—every dollar, one by one, until he was content with the amount.

He would usually do the task alone, but he knew that Illiana posed no threat. She wasn't your average woman. She did not need to steal, because she had her own, and her bank account was filled with endless zeroes. It was for this reason alone that he allowed her to be present.

After many lonely nights, Illiana's presence in Miami had become surprisingly welcomed. She was a distraction, someone he felt comfortable enough around because she understood his world. At first Zyir was hesitant to keep her too close, but after many lonely nights, the feelings of isolation and the ghosts that haunted his mind became too much. He needed companionship, and the time he spent with Illiana became convenient for Zyir.

Her warm body filled the empty space in his bed most nights, but unfortunately for Illiana, his heart remained ice cold. That was a void that only one woman could fill, and he had closed it off to the rest of the world the day that Breeze had been kidnapped. The day that she disappeared was the same day that Zyir gave up on love. Hustling was all that mattered, getting money his only concern. Even a woman as strikingly beautiful as Illiana could not soften his reserve. She had managed to squeeze into his bed, but he would never allow another woman to enter his life in the magnitude that Breeze Diamond had. Meeting her had changed the man that he was, and losing her had killed his spirit.

No, I can't afford to feel like that again. Loving a woman hurts too bad, he thought as he watched Illiana carefully.

"Why are you looking at me like that, papi?" Illiana asked, snapping Zyir out of his daze. "You see something you like?" Her flirtatious nature surfaced as she threw the money from her hands up into the air.

"What you doing, ma? You're fucking up the count," he objected with dismay.

Illiana shrugged her shoulders as she began to unbutton the shirt she was wearing, revealing her perky breasts and quarter-sized nipples.

"You're just going to count it again anyway," she said as she brought her face close to his and kissed his lips. Zyir turned his head, allowing her kisses to fall on his neck. Having a woman's lips on his own was too intimate for him. You kiss those that you love, and there was nothing but lust between them.

He flipped her over so that he was on top, and tapped her ass slightly. She already knew that he wanted to hit her from the back. He liked to see her derrière jiggle as he slid in and out of her.

Illiana was willing to give Zyir anything he desired. She was desperate to become his and to be affiliated with everything concerning him. She had never dealt with a man like him before. Everything about him attracted her, and she was pulling out all the stops in order to appeal to him. She wanted to be down, and the fact that he was a business associate of her brother's was even better. It meant that he was powerful because the Garza Cartel only dealt with the elite.

As he slid into her, she grimaced from his size, but with each stroke he put down on her, the pain slowly gave way to pleasure. She threw her pussy on him as if her life depended on it. There was no slow lovemaking going on. Zyir was beating it up. Illiana moaned loudly, unable to contain herself. He reached around her body and fingered her clit simultaneously, making her call out to him in Spanish. It didn't take her long to cum. Zyir was well versed in the female persuasion, and brought her to an orgasm better than any man before him ever could.

Money stuck to her sweat-covered body as she breathed in heavily from their intense escapade. She collapsed on the bed, exhausted as she watched Zyir stand before her.

"Come lay with me," she said as she rubbed the empty spot next to her. She saw the look in his eyes and knew that he was about to tell her no. She knew she had to turn up her game in order to get her way. He was constantly pulling away from her. Sex was her only weapon, the only thing that kept him near. "I'm not done with you yet," she said as she reached up and grabbed his penis. It came back alive instantly from her touch, and she smiled as she crawled to the edge of the bed and took him into her mouth. She was an expert at keeping a man interested in the bedroom. All she had to do was figure out how to keep Zyir focused on her once the sun came up. She wanted him for herself, and was willing to go to any extreme to ensure that he belonged to her.

Chapter Twelve

"I've killed niggas for less than what you've done."
–Carter

The Cartel had buried Breeze's memory so long ago that Carter did not believe his eyes. *This can't be her*, he thought as he rushed over to the bed and pulled the girl off of her knees.

"Hey! Wait your turn," the john protested. Carter pulled his gun and trained his aim on the man, who bitched up quickly, raising his hands in defense. He scrambled to get his clothing before scurrying out of the room.

"Breeze?" Carter called out. Breeze heard her name being called, but her high had her in a nod too deep to come out of.

"Carter, what is this? This is my place of business, señor. You can't just . . ."

The girl before him was a mere shell of the vibrant young woman he had come to know. His mind told him that this girl couldn't be Breeze. They had left her for dead so long ago and he was skeptical, but the resemblance was too similar to miss. When he saw the small gold cross hanging from her neck, her identity was confirmed. Through all of the storms that life had thrown her way, the necklace was still there. It had been the only piece of home she had left.

Carter turned his attention on Felipe as he rushed him with his gun drawn. He wrapped his hand around Felipe's throat as he put his gun directly to his forehead, forcing him against the wall of the bedroom. "Where'd you get her?" he barked as spit flew from his mouth.

Felipe could see that Carter was irrational. "I can see that you're upset over this girl—"

"She's my sister!" Carter shouted as he pulled back the hammer on his gun. "Where did you get her?" It would be his last time asking.

Carter knew that his actions were irrational and stupid, but he was acting out of emotion alone, disregarding the voice in the back of his mind telling him to calm down.

"Carter, this is not going to end well for you. I understand your reaction, and I can assure you that I had no idea of her affiliation to your family. Now that I know, something can be worked out," Felipe stated calmly yet firmly.

Carter released Felipe and rushed back over to Breeze. She was delusional as she reached up and wrapped her arms around his neck.

"Come here, baby. Let me make you feel good," she whispered, thinking that Carter was a john.

Pure emotion pulsed through him as he scooped her into his arms. Seeing her like this was breaking down the very essence of his manhood, making him feel weaker than he ever had before. He had failed her, Mecca had failed her, every man in her life who was supposed to keep her safe had failed.

"This ain't for you, Breeze," he stated sadly. "None of this was ever supposed to happen to you." Carter carried her over to Felipe, her head resting upon his broad shoulders as she fell into a nod.

"I'll buy her," Carter said. "A half a million dollars." There was no negotiating this bargain, and Felipe could see that bartering was not an option. Carter was a man who was protecting his family. That connection had no boundaries. Felipe knew this, because he would go against a thousand armies to ensure the safety of his own loved ones.

Felipe nodded and placed a hand on Carter's shoulder. He was not willing to give her away. To him, Breeze was just property, an expensive piece of real estate, but to maintain the business he was establishing with The Cartel, he was willing to sell her back. "If I could give her back to you for free, I would, but I paid a high price for her. A half a million dollars is not necessary. Just replace the seventy-five thousand dollars I spent in acquiring her and you can take her home," Felipe said.

Felipe opened the bedroom door. As Carter stepped out, he was instantly surrounded by Mexican men who held automatic machine guns pointed his way. He had no idea that Felipe had so many soldiers throughout the brothel. They were his security, and every room was monitored.

Felipe knew that he had never been in danger. The only person whose life was at stake was Carter's. Felipe lifted his hand to halt his army of loyal shooters, and shook his head from side to side.

"Let them pass," he said. Felipe turned to Carter. "My driver will take you back to the airstrip. I know you are eager to get home. We will take care of the details later."

The men lowered their weapons obediently, and Carter carried Breeze out of the brothel as she clung to him. He kissed the top of her head as he stepped into Felipe's limousine. When he was inside of the tinted vehicle, he broke down over Breeze, cradling her closely and hugging her tightly as his tears fell relentlessly. There was no stopping them. This was his baby sister, the most innocent one of them all, and yet she had been through the worst hell imaginable. The rest of his family had played the game and accepted the risks, but it was Breeze who had been sucked in by association, only to be chewed up and spit out. He could only imagine the cold and lonely place that she had just come from.

As he looked down at her face, he noticed the change in her. Whatever she had been through, it had drained her spirit. Even through the high from the heroin, he could see the hopelessness in her eyes. He grimaced as he thought of all of the men who had invaded her body, and as she began to scratch herself in her sleep, he saw the tell-all signs of a junkie.

As they pulled up to the airstrip and boarded the private jet, Carter held onto her tightly, as if she would disappear.

Breeze opened her eyes slightly and looked drowsily up at her older brother. "I just want to go home. Please take me to my family. They don't even know I'm alive," she whispered, still disoriented and unaware of her surroundings.

"I'm taking you home, Breeze, and nobody will ever hurt you again."

Zyir awoke to the sound of his cell phone vibrating against his wooden nightstand. He sat up and wiped the sleep out of his eyes as he reached over Illiana to answer it. Carter's name appeared on the screen, and he answered it immediately.

"Yo, fam, it's like seven in the morning. You know the streets don't see me until noon," Zyir stated with fatigue.

"I'm outside of your building. Buzz me in. We need to talk," Carter stated. Zyir had known Carter long enough to know when something serious had gone down.

"I thought you weren't due back from Tijuana until—"

"Open the door, Zy. I'll explain when I see you," Carter replied. His tone was demanding, but Zyir knew Carter too well not to pick up on the anxiety that was in his voice.

Zyir hung up his phone and then slid out of the bed to avoid waking Illiana. It was obvious that Carter wanted to discuss business, and he wanted the conversation to remain private. He shut his bedroom door as he exited and buzzed Carter in.

When Zyir opened the door and saw the stress lines on Carter's forehead, he knew something had gone awry. His red, sorrow-filled eyes told a story all their own.

"I need to talk to you," Carter stated as he stepped inside. Carter knew how Zyir felt about Breeze, and although her return was a joyous event, he wanted to prepare Zyir for it. He knew that Zyir loved his younger sister, and he did not want her condition to be a surprise to him. Breeze was not the same girl she used to be.

"No doubt, fam. Come in," Zyir invited as he stepped to the side to allow Carter to enter.

"It's about Breeze," Carter started.

"Breeze?" Zyir repeated in confusion. "Breeze is dead. We said our good-byes to her a long time ago."

"She's alive, Zyir," Carter stated as he put his hand on Zyir's shoulder.

Zyir smacked his hand away. It was the first time that he had ever bossed up against his mentor. His face frowned in pain as he backed away from Carter, bumping into his end table and sending a lamp crashing to the floor. The mere mention of Breeze's name was a soft spot for Zyir.

"Fuck is you saying, fam? She's been gone for almost two years! She's dead. We held the service . . ."

Carter stood stoically as he nodded his head. He knew that Zyir would take Breeze's reemergence just as hard as he had taken her actual death. "I know. We were wrong. She was still alive."

Zyir began to tear up as he put his hands on his head. "Don't say that to me, man. That means I gave up on her, fam. If she's been out there all this time, then I failed her. I was supposed to bring her home," Zyir stated emotionally as he punched the wall in frustration, putting his fist through the plaster and causing his knuckles to bleed.

He put his balled fists to the sides of his head in utter turmoil as he closed his eyes in horror. This was the last thing he had expected to hear Carter say. Wars he was ready to fight, money he knew how to collect, beef he enjoyed to cook, but to hear that the only girl he had ever loved had come back from the dead had him shook. It was the only situation that he was unprepared to handle. It was a chapter that he had closed in his life, and now it was about to be rewritten.

Zyir's grief reminded Carter of his own. It was the same way he felt about Miamor. He wished that she would magically reappear the same way that Breeze had done, but there was no bringing her back. She was gone forever, and because of this, he hoped that Zyir appreciated the gift that he was being given.

"She was working in one of Felipe's brothels. He says he purchased her from a woman who runs a human trafficking camp called Murderville. I don't know what Breeze has been through, but I know that she needs you."

Zyir looked at Carter in utter astonishment as he collapsed onto the couch. He buried his face in his hands and shook his head from side to side. His brain could not process the information, but his heart had sped up dramatically and felt as if it would beat out of his chest.

"Take me to her," Zyir stated.

"Take you to who?" Illiana's voice broke through the conversation and was an unwelcomed intrusion. She wasn't shy, and she made no efforts to cover her scantily clad body as she stood in front of Carter and Zyir while smoking a freshly rolled blunt.

Zyir ignored her question and refocused on Carter. "I need to see her, fam."

Carter saw the look of displeasure that crossed Illiana's face. He hoped that Zyir could see the signs that Illiana was giving off. It was obvious that she wanted more than Zyir was willing to give. The jealous look on Illiana's face spoke volumes, and Carter made a note to put Zyir up on game later.

"Handle your business and wrap things up here. I'll be waiting downstairs. Breeze will be happy to see you," Carter replied.

As Zyir dressed, Illiana stood in the doorway of his bedroom while smoking the cush weed slowly. *I know he's not rushing out to see some bitch when he has me here. Ain't nothing better than this,* Illiana thought arrogantly.

"Who is this Breeze bitch you're so worked up over?" Illiana asked.

Zyir stopped dead in his tracks and approached her as he buttoned up his Armani cardigan. He stood two inches away from her face as he said, "Don't ask questions about things that don't concern you. You're here to keep track of your brother's money, so start counting," Zyir stated, referring to the money that they had sexed on the night before. Without another word, he walked out of the room. Illiana's feelings were not his concern. He had one thing and one thing only on his mind—getting to Breeze.

"Thank you for meeting me," Mecca stated as he sat down on the park bench next to Leena and his nephew. She looked up at him and noticed the graze wound on his face. She had known him long enough to be able to tell that it had come from a bullet, one that had barely missed him.

"What happened to your face?" she asked.

"I had a little run-in with someone. Nothing major. I appreciate you showing up, Lee," he said, changing the subject.

"You said you had something to say," she replied. Leena was so short with him. She could not let go of the tiny piece of anger she still held onto, and Mecca heard it in her voice.

"You still toting pistols in my nephew's diaper bag?" Mecca asked, trying to lighten the mood.

Leena ignored his question as she looked out at the children playing in front of her. "What do you want, Mecca?" she asked impatiently.

"I don't know," Mecca replied honestly. "I want us to become friends again if that's possible."

Leena raised her eyebrows skeptically. "Friends?" she repeated.

"I know that's a lot to ask for, but it's the truth. I did what you said. I asked God for forgiveness."

"That's good, Mecca. I'm glad you took that first step," she admitted. She looked into his troubled eyes and said, "I wish you had taken it a long time ago."

"How do I know if it worked?" Mecca asked sincerely.

Leena looked at him suspiciously. She had never seen this side of Mecca before. "You will start to feel better," she replied. As she looked down at her son, who had fallen asleep in her lap, she said, "He looks just like you."

Mecca nodded and replied, "Money was always the winner. He was a lucky man."

"You were too, Mecca. You just didn't appreciate me like you should have," Leena admitted. The crowded, public place put her at ease around Mecca. She had snuck out while Estes was out playing golf, but she didn't dare meet Mecca in private. She chose a place where there would be too many witnesses for Mecca to try anything stupid.

"I appreciate you now," Mecca replied. "I'm tired of living recklessly, Lee. I know I've made a lot of mistakes in the past, but I need your help to make my future better. I have no right to ask you this, but you're the only person who can make me better. I don't want this life no more, ma."

Leena hated the fact that her heart raced around Mecca, but she could not stop it.

Just as she was about to respond, Mecca's phone rang loudly. He answered it.

"Yo, Mecca, you need to come to my place right away. It's important," Carter stated.

"I'm kind of in the middle of something," Mecca protested.

"It can wait," Carter insisted before hanging up the phone.

Mecca sighed as he turned back toward Leena. "I have to go, but I want to finish this discussion. Can we meet again?" he asked.

Against her better judgment, Leena nodded. "Yeah, Mecca. I'll meet you whenever you call."

It was a small step, but Mecca was grateful because it meant that it was possible for him to close the gap between them.

When Zyir saw Breeze lying in the bed, his knees almost gave out. The dark circles around her eyes, the track marks on her arms, and the bruises and cuts on her body made him cringe as if he could feel her pain. He sat in the chair next to her bed as Carter stood near the doorway.

"They doped her up," Zyir whispered, grief stricken as he grabbed her limp hand and held onto it gently. He kissed it and noticed that she was ice cold. She was in such bad condition that he almost didn't believe she was alive, but the rise and fall of her chest, along with the weak pulse he felt, told him otherwise. "What did they do to you, B? I'm sorry," he whispered.

He felt her stir slightly in her sleep as she began to come to. Her eyes opened, and she began to panic at the sight of the unfamiliar setting. She sat up in bed and put her back against the wall as she prepared to defend herself, but when her eyes met Zyir's, a sense of safety fell over her.

"You're not real," she uttered.

"I'm real, ma," he assured her as he reached out to touch her cheek.

She looked around in bewilderment. "I'm home?" she asked. "This is real?"

"Yeah, you're home, Breeze. You're safe now," Zyir stated. Breeze fell into his embrace as she wept heavily on his shoulder.

"I should have been there," Zyir said.

Breeze was too hysterical to respond. She choked on her own tears as Zyir held her tightly. Words would only complicate the situation, because neither of them could express how they were feeling.

It was the first time in his adult life that Zyir had allowed himself to cry. The love of a woman had made him whole again. Just seeing her face uplifted him. "I'm not letting you go, ma . . . ever. You hear me?" he stated as he held onto her tightly. "Tell me you trust me, ma. I'm sorry. I'm so sorry," he repeated over and over again.

"I trust you, Zyir," she whispered, absorbing his presence. She sucked it all in, because she was sure that at any moment she would wake up and it would all be a dream.

Mecca knocked on Carter's door, and when he saw his brother's face, he immediately became concerned.

"What happened? What's so urgent?" he asked.

"I found Breeze," Carter revealed. Mecca's eyes opened wide with hope as he raced past Carter and went from room to room until he finally located her in the spare bedroom. He stopped in his tracks when he saw her weeping passionately in Zyir's arms. He noticed her track-ridden arms immediately and winced in internal pain.

"Breeze," he called out to her, causing her to look up.

"Mecca!" she yelled as she jumped up and leaped into his arms. She wrapped her legs around his entire midsection as if she were still a little girl. He rubbed her hair and rocked her back and forth. He held onto his sister so tightly that she could not breathe, but she did not protest.

This feeling of familiarity, of safety, felt too good to Breeze. She had been deprived of her family for too long, and now she was back. It was too much for her to handle as she sobbed into Mecca's shoulder.

"Shh, it's okay now, B," he whispered as he held back his own tears. His efforts to stay strong failed him as tears began to fall from his eyes. "I'm going to kill a nigga. Everybody who ever hurt you, Breeze, I promise," he pledged as he felt her heart beating through her chest. "I thought you were gone, Breeze. I thought you were lost forever."

"They hurt me, Mecca. Over and over again," she cried.

"They're dead, B. Don't even think about that," Mecca said soothingly. He wiped his eyes as he held onto her. She was so weak that he had to be her strength. There was no room for him to be fragile. Breeze needed him, and as he caressed her hair soothingly, he gritted his teeth from the very thought of the abuse she had suffered. He had never been as gentle with anyone as he was with his baby sister at that moment. The Diamond family had kept her the most sheltered. She was their world.

The excitement of being home overwhelmed her, and her stomach began to boil as she realized how long it had been since her last fix. A full twenty-four hours had gone by, and to an addicted Breeze, that felt like a lifetime. She was used to being high around the clock.

"I'm going to be sick," she gurgled as she released Mecca. Zyir grabbed a small trash bin that sat beside the bed and rushed to her side as she threw up. Violent fits of vomit spewed from her mouth as Mecca watched in agony.

He knew that her body was craving heroine. He had been in the streets for too long not to notice the symptoms. Breeze was a dope head. His beautiful baby sister had been turned out, and the dismay he felt was written in agony on his face.

"I got her," Zyir stated, knowing that Mecca was about to break down any second.

Zyir laid Breeze back down in the bed as Mecca nodded and walked out of the room. It was too much for him to bear to see Breeze in so much distress.

Carter stared callously at Mecca as he entered the living room, and an uncomfortable silence filled the space between the two. He walked over to his wet bar and poured two glasses of cognac. He handed one to Mecca.

Mecca hesitantly took the drink from his brother as he stared at him intently. "Is it safe to drink?" Mecca asked directly.

"Why wouldn't it be?" Carter shot back.

As the two men sat waiting for Zyir to finish his time with Breeze, they did not speak, but the silence spoke louder than any words ever could. This reunion was supposed to be joyous, but there was a great divide between the two brothers that put a thick fog over the mood.

"Fuck it, nigga, let's get everything out in the open and lay the cards on the table. I know you know I killed your bitch," Mecca stated bluntly as he put his hand conveniently on his waistline near his .45.

"You gon' shoot me like you shot Monroe?" Carter countered, unrattled by Mecca. Carter had never been afraid of another nigga a day in his life, and the loose cannon in front of him was no exception. The safety on Carter's pistol was already off, and by the time Mecca chambered a round he would already be circled in chalk, if he wanted to play it that way. As Carter stared at Mecca, his nostrils flared in anger, but he kept his composure.

"That was a mistake," Mecca stated.

"I should have killed you. I've killed niggas for less than what you've done, but you're my brother, Mecca. I'm not like you. Loyalty is everything to me. If you had been any other nigga, I would have blown your brains out of your fucking head," Carter stated, enunciating each word so that Mecca understood him clearly. He paused as he stared intently at Mecca.

"Then why didn't you?" Mecca asked as he removed his .45 and placed it on his lap, his finger wrapped around the trigger, just in case. He did not want to have to shoot Carter, but there was malice in the air, and he knew that if he gave Carter the chance to bust first, it was over.

"Because you're not any other nigga. You are my blood, and having Breeze back has brought some perspective into my life. Family is all there is. Our sister is in that room right now, suffering because of a war you started . . . because of a lie that you told. We are the last three standing, and because of that, I cannot kill you. My sister . . . our sister loves you and she needs you. It is because of her and because of her only that I am willing to leave the past in the past."

"Everybody wanna label Mecca the bad guy," Mecca stated as he hit his chest and put his gun away. "You think this family isn't everything to me?" he asked. "I was out of my mind when I shot Money. I never meant for him to die, but you can't point fingers, Carter, because if family was so important to you, then you would have watched the company you kept."

"I'm not in the mood to decipher riddles. If you got something to say, just say it," Carter replied.

"That bitch Miamor! Open your eyes! She was just like me.

She poisoned my mother, and her fucking Murder Mamas tried to kill me."

"Don't put falsehoods on a ghost, Mecca. As a matter of fact, don't even speak her name," Carter stated harshly. It was too soon for Mecca to even try to justify his actions. Thinking of Miamor was like pouring alcohol on an open wound for Carter. It was excruciating.

"See, that's the shit I'm talking about! The truth has been in front of your face the entire time. You don't want to see it! You were fucking the enemy, and I wouldn't be surprised if you were just a mark to her all along. The bitch was a killer—a damned good one, too," Mecca stated with an ironic chuckle. "I did what you would have never been able to do! I protected this family, no matter the cost, so you can blame me all you want, but let me ask you this question: If I didn't kill her, who would she have killed next?"

Zyir came into the room and cleared his throat, interrupting the heated conversation. "She needs to be checked out by a doctor," Zyir said.

"I have a private physician coming here first thing in the morning," Carter informed. "She's out there bad. It's going to take a while for her to readjust and get the drugs out of her system. They were feeding her heroin three times a day, every day, in Mexico. We will all have to keep a very close watch over her."

"She's not staying here," Mecca spoke up. There was no way he was going to let anything happen to Breeze again. Anyplace where Miamor used to rest her head was not safe enough for his little sister. "She'll be safer at my place."

"She's not staying with you," Carter said with authority. There was no way he was entrusting her life to Mecca. "We both know what you're capable of."

"Fuck is that supposed to mean?" Mecca shouted defensively. He didn't appreciate the subtle jabs that Carter was taking at him. There was no way he would ever bring harm to Breeze.

"Means what it means, Mecca. She's not staying with you," Carter countered.

Just as an argument was about to break out, Zyir interjected. "She'll stay with me." The tone of his voice left no room for argument. Both Mecca and Carter respected Zyir. It was the best place for Breeze to recuperate safely.

Mecca grabbed his jacket and brushed past Carter as he headed for the door. "I'll be by to see Breeze tomorrow, Zyir. Keep her safe," he said sincerely.

Zyir nodded, and Mecca walked out without acknowledging Carter as he slammed the door forcefully behind him.

Zyir looked at Carter curiously. "Fuck was that all about?" he asked.

Carter shook his head as worry lines creased his forehead. He downed the rest of his drink before replying, "He killed Miamor."

Although Zyir had a million questions to ask, he knew that if Carter wanted him to know details, he would have elaborated. Without hesitation, Zyir answered, "You want me to handle that?"

Carter sighed, wishing that the solution could be so easy. He poured himself another drink. "There's nothing to handle. He's my brother. I can't give that order after everything that this family has been through. Just take care of Breeze, Zy. That's all I need from you right now. You're the only person who I can trust at the moment. Everybody else in this fucking city has been wearing a mask all along."

Chapter Thirteen

"The line between the two is so thin that I go back and forth every day."

–*Leena*

Zyir paced anxiously back and forth outside the closed bedroom door as the doctor examined Breeze inside. Worrying over her condition was heart wrenching. He had no idea what she had gone through, and he only hoped that the damage she had suffered could be repaired. The nervousness and gut-bubbling concern that he felt for her was almost unbearable. He felt an overwhelming responsibility to rehabilitate Breeze, to restore her to the beautiful, unscathed young woman she used to be. The love he had for her extended that of girl-friend/boyfriend. He felt obligated to her just as much as he was to himself. It was as if they were one and just by looking into her eyes, he had absorbed all of her pain; he shared it with her and knew that he had to help her heal. Finding her had only been half the battle. The other half was yet to come.

Illiana watched Zyir in silent disgust as she fumed on the inside. *All of a sudden this Breeze bitch comes home and he acts like I don't even exist,* she thought irritably. *The junkie bitch ain't even all that. What the hell does he see in her?*

She had no idea just how deeply Zyir's affection ran for Breeze, but seeing him completely absorbed in her was enough to make Illiana green with envy. It was the attention she craved from him. The love she was scheming to get. Rejection was something she had never learned to take, and Breeze being back in the picture only complicated things for her.

"Why don't you come to bed, Zyir? It's three o'clock in the morning, papi," she said as she walked up on him and wrapped her arms around his neck. Her blood red painted nails scratched him softly with every caress. Staring into his eyes, it seemed as if he had aged overnight. He was carrying the burdens of a man twice his age, and they were evident in the frown lines that creased his brow.

He shook his head and removed her arms from around him. "Go ahead and get your rest, ma. I'm going to wait to speak with the doctor. I have to find out what happened to her, and I need to make sure she's okay," Zyir replied.

Displeased with his lack of attention, Illiana rolled her eyes and sighed angrily as she retreated to Zyir's bedroom.

Zyir ignored the little show she was putting on. *She's not my chick, just someone to pass the time with. I've never given her a reason to think this is anything more than what it is,* he justified in his head.

He didn't want Illiana to become too attached because now that Breeze was back, he knew that one day he was going to have to let Illiana go. He would just have to use tact and be careful with the way he ended things. Illiana was more connected than an interstate highway, and he didn't want to cross those who she had ties to.

I'ma have to play that situation right. Can't have a scorned woman fucking up business, Zyir thought.

The doctor finally emerged from his guest bedroom, breaking Zyir from his thoughts.

"Yo, Doc, how is she?" Zyir asked in a low tone. Breeze's condition wasn't everyone's business. He did not want Illiana, or even Breeze herself, to overhear the prognosis.

"After a full physical and vaginal exam, I found that she is in overall good health considering where she was found. A lot of girls coming from her circumstances contract incurable diseases. She is one of the lucky ones. I did find a lot of tearing and bleeding, which leads me to believe that she's been raped repeatedly for some time now.

"I found antibiotics in her system. Wherever she was, they kept her clean so that she would not infect their clientele with any sexually transmitted diseases. That alone may have saved her life.

"She has a lot of contusions and bruised bones. I even found a hairline fracture on the back of her skull. Those things will heal with time and a lot of rest. There are high levels of heroin in her system, however. She needs to be admitted to a rehab facility immediately. I can recommend some if you would like," the doctor said.

The more the man spoke, the more dismayed Zyir became. It seemed that every part of Breeze was scarred. His chest tightened as he thought of the men who had violated her and of the abuse she had been forced to endure; all the while, the people who loved her, himself included, had moved on without her.

As Zyir walked the doctor to the door, he relived the moment that he had slipped up and she had been kidnapped. It had been the worst day of his life. The doctor could see the turmoil on his face.

"Thank you for coming and for all of your help," Zyir stated as he went into his pocket and handed the doctor a decent-sized knot of crisp hundred dollar bills. "We appreciate your professionalism and discretion."

The doctor knew that Zyir spoke on behalf of the greatest criminal enterprise in the state of Florida. He nodded his head in acknowledgement, but before he was all the way out the door, he said, "My greatest concern for Breeze is her mental stability. She won't talk about what she's seen or been through, which leads me to believe that it is too traumatic to relive. I strongly urge you to watch her closely, twenty-four hours a day if you have to."

"Suicide watch?" Zyir questioned.

The doctor nodded grimly and replied, "Unfortunately, yes. She is going to need a lot of support. She needs to regain her physical health as well as her mental health. No one but Breeze knows the things that she's been through, so handle her with extreme care."

Zyir watched the doctor leave and then made his way to Breeze's bedside. She slept restlessly. Sweat covered her body and she twitched involuntarily as the potency of her last high passed out of her. Zyir got on his knees and grabbed Breeze's hand as he put his head down. He didn't want to wake her, only to let her know that he was right beside her and he wasn't going anywhere.

Illiana awoke to the loneliness of an empty bed and frowned. The undisturbed sheets let her know that Zyir hadn't been beside her all night. She climbed out of bed and pulled one of his shirts over her head before she went searching for him. Tiptoeing through the house in the dark with ease, she crept to the door of the guest bedroom.

Zyir was so unaware of anything and everyone except Breeze that he did not notice Illiana standing behind him. The delicate way in which he touched her made Illiana sick. There was no misinterpreting his actions toward her.

He loves this girl, Illiana thought as she scoffed and crossed her arms. She walked back to the bedroom knowing that with Breeze Diamond in the picture, she would never secure a spot in Zyir's world.

I have to get rid of her, she thought as she climbed back into bed. It was the only solution.

Illiana's features were so striking that they appeared deadly. As the wheels of manipulation began to turn in her pretty little head, she smiled deviously. These were exactly the type of games she loved to play. There was only room for one woman in Zyir's life, and she was determined to make sure that she was it.

Leena lay in bed with the silky sheets wrapped around her gorgeous physique as if she were a Greek goddess. Her mind spun wildly as thoughts of Mecca filled her head. Her son lay beside her, and Estes rested on the other side of him. On the outside they looked like a happy family, but on the inside, she yearned for something more, something irresistible, something dangerous—and that something was a new life with Mecca Diamond.

Don't be stupid Leena! He shot you. Don't go there. Stop thinking with your heart and use your head, she told herself. She could not understand how she could still care for the man who had tried to end her life, but her heart was a puzzle that was too complicated to piece together. It wanted what it wanted, and the more she reacquainted herself with Mecca, the more she wanted him.

There was something about the Diamond mystique that always pulled her in. She had felt the same thing with Monroe, and now that Mecca seemed to be changing, he was magnetic to her as well.

She was so conflicted, so torn over him. Everything in her wanted to hate him. He deserved to be punished for the acts of sin he had committed against her, but seeing his transformation made it easier to forgive. He was slowly changing into a better man. She had known Mecca for a long time and knew that it would not be easy for him to give up the life he had been born into, but he was trying, and that alone impressed her.

The ticking of the antique grandfather clock in the corner of the room kept her awake as her heart raced in the midnight hour. *How can you still love him?* She asked herself, but she knew that she loved Mecca because it was the next best thing to loving Monroe. They were so much alike that she could not keep up her angry visage toward Mecca. Every time she saw his face she remembered Monroe. Identical in every way except demeanor, Mecca and Monroe were two halves that made up her whole heart. Those two halves equaled the one true love of her life.

Hesitantly, she sat up in bed and peeked over at Estes. His light snoring indicated that he was in a deep sleep. She took a deep breath as she leaned down to kiss her son's cheek before she slid out of bed. She knew that the decision she was about to make could be detrimental to her health.

I have to see him, she thought as she slipped on her clothes, moving silently through the dark as she dressed. She grabbed her Chanel bag and fished out her keys as she snuck out of the door, hoping that Estes would not awaken before she returned.

Fear, anxiety, and anticipation filled her as she pulled away from Estes' home. She pulled out her cell phone and dialed Mecca's number.

"Mecca, I need to see you," she said as soon as he answered.

Without hesitation, he gave her his address, and she sped through the city streets, her Benz making its way to Mecca's place in record speed. She sat in front of his building for an hour, listening to the pattern of the rain falling on the roof of her car. It was as if the sky were crying right along with her as her own tears flowed down her cheeks.

Confusion plagued her as she tried to make sense of her feelings. Knowing that Mecca was no good, she started to leave, but every time she went to put the car in drive, she froze. She needed to see Mecca, and although the consequences of her actions would be great, she decided to stay.

She got out of the car before she lost her nerve, and ran into the high-rise building. Her throat felt as if it would close as she took the elevator to the penthouse on the top floor, and nervous energy filled her.

She went to Mecca's door and lifted her hand to knock, but before she could, Mecca pulled it open. He stood before her, shirtless, with a blunt in one hand, as weed smoke danced in the space around him.

She took in everything about him. Mecca was a beautiful man. From his broad and well-sculpted chest to his strikingly handsome features, he was perfect. His only flaw was his dangerous temper. She had seen it firsthand. It had almost cost her everything, yet there she stood, intrigued and forgiving in front of him.

Overwhelmed by his presence, she stopped thinking and did what felt right to her: she kissed him passionately, catching Mecca off guard as she backed him into the penthouse. Their pace was feverish as desire filled the space between them.

Mecca fumbled to put out the blunt without breaking their connection. "I'm so sorry, Lee," he whispered over and over again in her ear, causing her tears to flow.

Hearing the sincerity in his words was like a punch to the gut as she pushed him away. "Why did you have to speak, Mecca? Why did you have to remind me of what you did? Every time you apologize, I remember that night!" she yelled as she put her hands to her face and turned toward the door.

"Leena—"

Before Mecca could get his words out, she stalked over to

him in a rage and slapped him across the face. "I hate you, Mecca. I hate you for what you did!!" she yelled, her anger ablaze in her emotion-filled eyes.

"Then why are you here?" he asked as he touched the side of her face. The gentleness that he displayed was uncharacteristic for him. This new version of Mecca that stood before her was so much easier to love than the callous gangster she knew him to be.

She sobbed as if she were ashamed of herself. She replied, "Because I love you. The line between the two is so thin that I go back and forth every day."

Mecca embraced her, and she fought him as she tried to regain control of her heart.

"No, Mecca, I have to go. I shouldn't have come here. What the fuck was I thinking? I have to think of my son," she protested.

"Stop fighting me, ma," he whispered. He took her chin into his hand and lifted her face to his, kissing her gently. She melted as she kissed him back, indulging in the forbidden affection she felt for him.

"I'm trying, Leena. I'm trying to change. You don't know how much I wish I could take back—"

"Don't," she said as she looked up at him. "Don't keep making me relive it, Mecca. We can't take back the things we did in the past, and it's too painful for me to think about. I know that being here with you is a mistake, but please just let me make it."

"Okay," he replied simply as he picked her up, her long legs wrapping around his body as he placed his hands on her behind. He carried her to his bedroom as their tongues performed a delicate dance. He laid her down on his bed and then stood up as he admired her.

Seeing her in his bed, alive and breathing, caused him

much distress as he felt his chest swell. Although he had hurt Leena, she had hurt him as well. She was a constant reminder of the monster he had become. At that moment, everything sexual about their interaction went out of his mind. His motive was different. What he sought from her was intimacy. He wanted to feel the unconditional love that she had for him.

As he looked down at her, his heart swelled, and for the first time in his life, he was selfless, thinking of her before himself. After everything he had done to her, Leena still came back to him. The hollow space inside his chest, where his heart should have dwelled, ached because he realized that he loved her too. He lay down beside her and pulled her close to his body.

"I just want to hold you, Lee. Just stay here with me. Forgive me, Leena," he whispered as he kissed the top of her head.

Leena closed her eyes as the heat from his body warmed her. She was reluctant in her decision, but knew that it was one she would still make, despite the warning bells ringing in her conscience. "I do, Mecca. I forgive you."

When Breeze opened her eyes, her entire body hurt. She had been asleep for three days straight, but now that she was awake and coherent, she felt the horrible effects of withdrawal. She reached for the IV that was in her arm and weakly pulled it out. As she stood to her feet, the weight of her body was unbearably heavy. Despite the fact that she had lost tremendous weight, it felt like her bones would break with every step that she took. Her body had been dependent on heroin for so long that it was no longer producing the endorphins she needed to resist pain. Every inch of her body hurt. The pressure of her feet hitting the floor felt as if she were walking on glass. It was no longer a matter of enjoying the high; she needed heroin to keep her functioning. Without it, she felt sick.

For so long she had convinced herself that she would never make it home. Now that she was back, she felt dirty and ashamed of where she had been. As she made her way out of the room, she gripped her churning stomach with one hand while keeping her balance against the wall with the other. When she stepped into the hallway, the smell of food cooking drew her to the kitchen.

She was caught off guard by the unfamiliar face that greeted her. Illiana stood in a Victoria's Secret negligee as she prepared breakfast. Breeze gasped at her beauty, and instantly began to smooth out her own hair from insecurity.

I used to look like that, she thought as she fumbled nervously, ashamed of her appearance.

When Illiana realized she had an audience, she smirked. "So, the famous Breeze Diamond does more than sleep," she said as she motioned her hand for Breeze to sit.

"W-where's Zyir?" Breeze asked as she sat down timidly, wincing from the pressure of her tailbone hitting the wooden chair. She looked around nervously as she shivered and rubbed the goose bumps on her bare arms. Being home felt odd, as if she no longer belonged, and the way Illiana was looking at her made her feel out of place.

"He's in the shower," Illiana replied as she looked Breeze up and down from head to toe. *I don't see what all the fuss is about,* she thought as she instantly judged Breeze.

"Who are you?" Breeze asked.

Illiana fixed herself a plate and began to walk past Breeze. She stopped right next to her and replied, "I'm the new bitch in Zyir's life that you don't want to fuck with." She placed the plate of food down in front of Breeze so hard that some of the food fell onto the table. "Here, you need this more than I do. You look like shit."

Feeling as if she hadn't eaten in days, she dug into the plate, as Illiana shook her head and walked away.

She's pathetic, she thought as she walked back into Zyir's bedroom.

"You cooking?" Zyir asked in surprise as soon as she came into the room. Water dripped from his rock hard abs, and the white towel that was hanging from his hips barely covered his family jewels as she eyed him hungrily.

"Don't act so surprised, Zyir. Our houseguest woke up, so I just thought I would make her something to eat. She looks so unhealthy," Illiana replied with fake innocence. "Your plate is on the stove."

Zyir nodded his head, but looked at her skeptically. "Play nice, Illiana. Now is not the time for bullshit," he warned.

"What?" she feigned. "Can't a girl do something nice?" she asked.

"Not a girl like you. Every move you make is calculated," Zyir answered as he finished dressing.

He bypassed Illiana as he went to join Breeze in the kitchen. He noticed that when he approached her, she wouldn't look him in the eyes. He walked right up on her and kneeled in front of her. Reaching up to touch her face, he felt his heart speed up. No matter how much she had changed, he was grateful to have her back. He had never thought he would see her alive again.

"You should be in bed, B," he whispered as he brushed a piece of food from the side of her delicate mouth.

"Where is everyone, Zyir? I just want my mother. Has she been to see me? Why am I not at home with her?" Breeze asked.

Zyir became silent. A lot had happened in Breeze's absence, and it had slipped his mind that she was unaware of her mother's death.

I can't tell her that, he thought. *She should hear it from Carter or Mecca.*

Breeze noticed the look of uncertainty in Zyir's eyes. "Where is she, Zyir? Where is my mother? I need her," she said in a pleading tone.

"She's gone. She died after you disappeared," he said, giving her the news as gently as possible.

Breeze reached out and gripped Zyir's shirt tightly as her head fell onto his chest. Her vision was so blurry with tears that she couldn't see as she cried silently. She could not even form the words to express the sharp pain that radiated through her heart.

"I know, B . . . I know," Zyir soothed as he rubbed her back.

"It just hurts so bad. I wasn't even here. I missed everything," Breeze cried.

"Nah, ma, everything missed you. Nothing has been the same since you've been gone. You're home now, and I'm gonna take care of you," Zyir assured. Zyir picked her up and carried her back into the guestroom.

"Aghh!" she whimpered as he lay her down. Even the thousand thread count sheets felt painful to her. She gripped his hand as he watched over her sympathetically. "Zyir, please . . . this hurts too bad. I need you to help me. Please just give me a little bit to make me feel better."

Hearing her beg him for dope broke his heart. He would do anything to take her pain away—anything except what she was requesting of him.

"I can't do that, Breeze. You don't need that, ma. I'm going to help you through this, but you've got to be strong," he said.

Breeze began to shake as a chill set into her bones, and she squirmed uncomfortably.

Tears of rage rushed Zyir, but he held them back, refusing to let even one fall. He dipped the sponge on the nightstand into a bowl of cold water and wiped it across her forehead. "What happened to you, ma?" he asked. "Tell me who did this to you. Who took you, Breeze?"

Breeze closed her eyes, because she knew that once she admitted what had occurred, Zyir and her family would never look at her the same.

"Talk to me, Breeze. You can tell me," Zyir urged. He was ready to pop off on anyone who had played a role in kidnapping Breeze.

"It was Ma'tee. I was trapped in Haiti with Ma'tee," she replied. Images of the constant rape raced through her mind as she shook her head from side to side, her eyes still closed from fear of the look that Zyir was giving her. "He raped me every day Zyir, and no matter how hard I try, I can't stop feeling his hands on my body."

Her revelation would not allow him to remain strong. He cried at her bedside as he gripped her hand and kissed her face repeatedly. "I'm going to murder that nigga, Breeze. You hear me? I'm going to—"

"He's already dead," she whispered. "The earthquake killed him. It was how I got away from him, but I only went from one hell to another."

It took everything in Zyir not to explode, and he turned away from Breeze so that she could not witness his grief.

"That's why I didn't want to tell you. You don't want me anymore," Breeze said.

Zyir cleared the tears from his face and gained his composure before turning around. "I'll always want you, Breeze, and you never have to talk about it again. You are home now, and that is all that matters. I'ma stick with you through it all, B, and I'll body anyone who ever hurts you again. All you have to do is promise me you'll try . . . try to kick this shit, Breeze. That's the one thing that I can't do for you. You have to want that for yourself."

Breeze nodded and replied, "I will, Zyir. I promise you I'll get clean."

As Illiana's prying ears eavesdropped on the conversation, she felt reassured. She had seen the effects that heroin could have over a person. Breeze was hooked, and Illiana was going to make sure that she stayed that way. Illiana's infatuation with Zyir was so strong that she never even considered how evil her actions toward Breeze would be. She was out for self; nobody else mattered.

Dawn came too early for Leena as the rising sun shone brightly through the floor to ceiling windows of Mecca's penthouse. She knew that she had stayed too long, but being wrapped up in Mecca's arms felt so good that she did not want to let him go.

She slid from beneath him and walked out onto the large balcony. She wished that she could stay there forever and just move forward without ever looking back, but her son kept her rooted with Estes. Estes was security, and although she did not love him, she knew that he had the means to provide her child with everything.

The purple and orange hues that blended in the sky relaxed her, and she sighed as she thought of how complicated her life had just become.

"Why did I come here?" she asked herself, knowing that she had just opened Pandora's box.

She felt Mecca walk up behind her, and her shoulders tensed as the hairs on the back of her neck rose in fear.

"Don't fear me, Lee. I'm trying to show you that I'm not a monster," he whispered into the back of her neck with his eyes closed as he inhaled her natural scent. He wrapped his arms around her waist and she relaxed.

"I know, Mecca. I'm trying. I just have to get used to this new you. You have to be patient with me. My trust in you isn't something that can be restored overnight."

The feeling of Mecca's lips on the nape of her neck caused her love box to throb in anticipation. It had been so long since she had been pleased. She wanted to slow things down, but the spot between her thighs had a different agenda. She gasped as Mecca's hands caressed her thighs, moving higher and higher until his fingers found her clit.

Without speaking, he moved with expertise as he spread her legs and removed his manhood. She felt the girth of him as he rubbed his thick head against her voluptuous behind. She dripped in anticipation. Nothing had ever felt so forbidden, yet she still craved it. She wanted him to put his thing down. The bedroom was the one place where his aggression never scared her.

Bending her over the thirty-five-story balcony, he parted her glistening southern lips and entered her from behind.

"You want me to stop?" he asked as he paused inside of her. He wanted her to be completely comfortable with what was about to go down.

"No," she replied. "Psst," she sighed as she felt every inch of him dig into her from behind.

Mecca's hand gripped the sides of her ass. Her wetness was like heaven to him. Her juicy peach fit snugly around his shaft as her muscles pulled him tighter and deeper with every stroke.

"Oooh, Mecca," she moaned as she bucked back on his dick, loving the mixture of pain and pleasure that he was giving her. Her head spun from orgasmic intoxication as she took in the scenery below. She could feel herself being sucked back into Mecca's world, but at that exact moment, she did not care.

If this is what it feels like, I wanna be here forever, she thought as her eyes closed in pleasure.

The morning air caused her nipples to harden as Mecca turned her around. She mounted him as he held her up with one hand and palmed her perky breasts with the other, all the while their tongues intertwined. It had been so long since a man had been inside of her. Estes had expressed his interest, but she could never bring herself to sleep with him, and now all of the sexual tension that she had built up was about to come down.

"I'm cumming," she whispered feverishly. "Ooh, Mecca, right there."

Mecca increased his pace as the tip of his dick swelled, and a tingle ran down his spine. "Me too, Lee. Shit, ma."

Mecca cried out in pleasure as he shot his load into her, but he did not stop pleasing her until she creamed all over him.

Exhausted, she fell into his chest. Her labored breathing filled the air. She didn't know what her next move would be, and she hid her face to avoid reality.

"Lee," he said as he lifted her chin. "I want you to leave him."

"I don't know if I can," she admitted honestly. "I owe him so much. He has been nothing but generous and kind to me."

"Are you happy?" he asked.

"Will I be happy with you?" she countered with raised eyebrows. She wanted him to reassure her, to convince her that she would be, but it was something that Mecca could not guarantee.

He lowered his gaze.

"Exactly. I didn't think so," she said sadly as she walked back into his penthouse.

Mecca listened as the shower ran in his master bathroom, and he sat down on his bed with his face in his hands. He was trying. He was doing all that he could to redeem himself, but he wasn't completely sure that he could purge himself of all the evil that lived inside of him. He wanted Leena. She held the key to his future, but he did not want to hurt her again.

As she emerged from his bathroom fully dressed, he knew that she was ready to walk out of his life.

She's better off with Estes, he thought as she headed directly to the door. The selfishness in him caused him to stop her.

"Leena . . ."

She paused mid-step and turned to him, revealing a tear-streaked face.

"Leave him. Come away with me," he said.

"My son," she protested.

"He has my blood in his veins, Leena. Let me raise him. I'll take care of you," he replied.

Leena wanted to say no because she knew that it was the right answer, but her heart would not listen to reason. She ran toward Mecca and kissed him passionately.

"Okay . . . okay, Mecca. Just let me do this on my own terms. I'll leave him, I swear."

"Leena, I'm leaving with or without you, but you would make my life so much better if you come," he admitted.

"Just tell me when and where to be. I'll be there. I'll leave with you," she said as she walked out the door.

Mecca watched her leave, but he was confident that she would soon be back. The game was getting old for him, and at that moment, all he wanted was to leave his old life behind so that he could start anew with Leena. She was slowly becoming his only priority—and even Estes could not keep him away from her.

Emilio Estes sat behind the dark tint of the Lincoln truck and held his great grandson in his arms as he watched Leena leave Mecca's building. Disappointment filled him as he kissed Monroe Jr.'s chubby cheeks. "I can't let your mother make this mistake," Estes said, more to himself than to the baby in his arms. "I told him to stay away."

He shook his head in disgust as he thought of how he would have to press the button on Mecca. He was a liability. As long as he was around, Leena would be drawn to him, and Estes was not giving her up, especially to his crooked grandson. Mecca was a ticking time bomb, and before he could explode again, Estes would kill him. This time, there would be no mercy. Mecca had to go.

Chapter Fourteen

"I stay strapped."
—Murder

Murder had been patiently waiting to see Mecca again. Murder had staked out Monroe's grave all Sunday morning, hoping to see Mecca there again, just as he had done one week before.

This nigga is bound to show up here sometime, he thought as he sat back. He thought about what the Murder Mamas had said about him taking a different approach in killing the remaining leaders of The Cartel. He knew that to do it, he would have to get in close with them so he could kill Zyir, Mecca, and Carter with ease. He didn't have the luxury of just killing one of them and being satisfied. In Miamor's honor, all of them had to go.

He looked across the cemetery and saw a tinted truck and knew that Robyn and Aries were waiting inside, strapped. He had a plan, and if everything went as expected, he would be in a better position by the end of the day.

Just as expected, Mecca's car rolled up slowly and parked. Mecca stepped out of the car, scanned the area, and checked his surroundings. Once he felt comfortable, he closed the door and headed toward Monroe's grave.

Murder hopped out of his car also and tried to look as casual as he could as he headed to the grave. Murder patted his hip to make sure his .40 caliber pistol was in place.

Mecca was on the path to the tombstone and didn't notice Murder walking a couple of feet behind him. Murder looked across the site and nodded, knowing the girls were watching closely and waiting for his signal to go through with the plan and get it popping.

On cue, tires began to screech and the sounds of gunfire erupted. The Murder Mamas had on ski masks, and Robyn had an assault rifle. She was hanging out of the window. Aries drove by while shooting her own handgun out of the window.

Murder quickly dove on Mecca, knocking him out of the way as he was taken by total surprise. Murder began to fire back, but he aimed high purposely, so he wouldn't hit Robyn and Aries.

The whole scenario was planned to a tee. It was done and over within fifteen seconds, but those fifteen seconds were instrumental in Murder's plans.

Mecca was taken off guard, and he had left his guns in the car, not thinking anything would pop off at a cemetery. He breathed hard as he saw Murder send bullets at the tinted car that was speeding out of the cemetery. Murder ran after the car, firing bullet after bullet until his clip was empty, showing Mecca that he wasn't scared.

"You good?" Murder asked as he looked back at Mecca, who was still on the ground.

"Yeah, I'm good," Mecca said as his heart beat rapidly. "Damn!" Mecca yelled as he thought about how his life had almost ended. "You saved my ass," Mecca added.

"Don't trip. I saw that shit coming from a mile away. I'm just glad that I had my strap on me. You must have an enemy somewhere, huh?" Murder said as he extended his hand to help Mecca up.

"Yeah, something like that. Thanks, fam," Mecca said as he stood up and dusted off his pants.

"Don't mention it," Murder said as he walked toward the tombstone as if the conversation was over.

"Yo, hold up," Mecca said as he followed Murder. "That was some real shit. What, you a cop or something?" Mecca asked, wondering why he would just be carrying a gun on him.

"Hell nah. I hate cops," Murder answered as he put his gun inside his holster. "I stay strapped, that's all."

"Yo, I'm Mecca," Mecca said as he extended his hand for a shake.

"I'm Leon, but my people call me Murder."

"Okay, Murder. Nice to meet you. Let me bless you for doing what you did." Mecca said as he reached into his pocket and pulled out a stack full of money.

"Nah, I'm good. You keep that. I just acted on impulse. It was nothing," Murder said.

"Well, at least let me buy you a drink," Mecca asked with a small smirk. He liked Murder's style and quick thinking. He knew that he could always use a live nigga around him. Murder impressed him just that quick.

"No doubt," Murder responded, accepting the invitation. Mecca had just fallen right into Murder's trap, and although Murder had a stone cold expression on his face, on the inside he was smiling, because he knew that the countdown to the end of The Cartel had just begun.

"And that's how I ended up in Miami," Murder said, just finishing a made-up story to Mecca. He told Mecca that he came from Atlanta searching for a coke connect, and had only been in town for a couple of months. Murder also told him that his father moved to Florida and had recently passed, which was something Mecca could relate to. Needless to say, they hit it off quickly.

Murder took a shot of Patrón and slammed the glass on the table. Mecca signaled the waiter to bring them another shot as they sat in the rear of a low-key bar that Mecca frequented. Murder's trigger finger was itching, and he wanted so badly to pull of his .40 and blow Mecca's head clean off, but he knew that he couldn't show his card this early in the game. Murder's hand began to sweat and he gritted his teeth, all while keeping on a smile in front of his enemy.

How can I be having a drink with the coward that killed my baby? Miamor was my mu'fuckin' heart. I should blow his head off right now, Murder thought as he casually slipped his hand down to his waist where his gun rested, locked and loaded. He quickly snapped back and thought about the bigger picture, and that was taking them all out.

"You say you looking for a coke connect, right?" Mecca said as he leaned in closer to Murder so that no one could overhear him.

"Yeah, that shit in Atlanta is so stepped on, and when we do get a good batch in, they taxing up the ass," Murder said.

"How about . . ." Mecca started, but stopped when the waitress came and set the two shots of Patrón on the table. He continued when she left. "How about I show you how to make some real money?" Mecca said as he leaned back and took the shot with no chaser.

"How can I do that?" Murder asked as he sat back looking very interested, knowing that Mecca was playing into his little trap.

"I saw the way you reacted out there today. I need a nigga like that on my team. You feel me?"

"I'm listening," Murder stated.

"I want you to be my enforcer, my bodyguard for a couple of months. I will also plug you in on some bricks when you go back to Atlanta. Unstepped on, raw," Mecca offered.

"Word?" Murder asked as he took his shot and looked Mecca in the eyes.

"Word!" Mecca said as he extended his hand, waiting for Murder to seal the deal.

Murder shook Mecca's hand, and thoughts of Miamor's horrific murder scene popped in his head. Murder's trigger finger began to itch again, and he gritted his teeth, feeling disgusted that he was shaking his own enemy's hand. Nevertheless, Murder stayed calm and didn't show his cards so soon. He knew that in due time, he would get his revenge in a major way.

Murder left that meeting feeling like in some way he had betrayed Miamor; however, he knew that to take down The Cartel correctly, he would have to play a role. Murder had just ordered the Murder Mamas to head back to L.A., and even though they were against leaving him there alone, Murder insisted. Murder had taught Miamor everything she knew about her profession, and off the strength of that, Robyn and Aries listened to him.

At that moment, Murder was on his way to meet Mecca at a warehouse, and the Murder Mamas were in the air headed home. On that day, Murder was supposed to meet Zyir and Carter for the first time. Murder questioned his willpower. He was not sure that he would be able to handle seeing Carter without reaching for his gun and going all out. Only time would tell.

Murder took a deep breath and whispered, "I love you, Miamor," as if she were in the car with him. Deep in his heart, he was confident that she could hear him.

As Murder pulled into the warehouse where Mecca had directed him to meet them, he took a deep breath to prepare himself. It was an old steel factory on the outskirts of Miami. The Diamond family owned the property, so it looked as if it was a shut down establishment, but it was where the bricks were stored and shipments were dropped off.

Murder stepped out of the car, and moments later, a Lamborghini pulled up behind him, shining its lights on him. Murder blocked his eyes and tried to see who the driver was. It wasn't until Mecca killed the lights and the butterfly-style door arose that Murder saw who it was.

"What's up, fam?" Mecca asked as he approached Murder.

Murder instinctively clenched his jaws as his hatred for Mecca surfaced once again. Murder caught himself and calmed down before Mecca got close enough to read the expression on his face. Niggas like Mecca could sense larceny, so Murder had to be sure to keep his temper in check at all times.

"What's good?" Murder said between clenched teeth. He shook Mecca's hand and put on a fake smile just before Mecca led him into the warehouse.

Carter and Zyir were already there, counting money and loading duffel bags with the bricks so that they could be distributed to their blocks. They had been there for over an hour and had parked in the back out of sight.

As Murder walked in, he had to stop his mouth from hitting the floor. He had never seen so many kilos of cocaine in his life. It was then that he knew that The Cartel was much more than street legend. They were the real deal.

Having Carter, Zyir, and Mecca in one place at the same time, he thought about taking them out right there. But he quickly changed his tune when he saw the arsenal of automatic weapons sitting on the table near the money.

"What took you so long?" Carter asked as he thumbed through the hundred dollar bills without looking up.

Zyir frowned when he saw the man following Mecca. "Fuck is this new nigga?" Zyir asked, not one to hold his tongue.

"I had to make a stop, but check it. This is my man I was telling you about. This nigga is on some Jet Li type shit with the pistols. He's nice," Mecca bragged.

"Word?" Carter said as he stood from the table to shake Murder's hand. Mecca had told Carter and Zyir about Murder, and they needed an enforcer, so they had wanted to meet him. But when Carter shook Murder's hand, he felt that something was off. Call it a hustler's intuition; the handshake wasn't right, the eye contact was too stiff, and Murder's body language didn't match his facial expression.

"Murder, this is Carter. Carter, Murder," Mecca said, introducing the two men that both loved Miamor to the bone.

"What's up?" Carter said.

"'Sup family?" Murder returned.

"And this is Zyir. He handles everything on the street level," Mecca said. Zyir was so busy counting the money that he didn't even properly greet Murder. Zyir just glanced at him briefly and nodded his head.

Carter didn't say anything then, but he made a mental note to tell Mecca to ditch the new nigga. He didn't get a good vibe from him, and rightfully so, because Murder wanted all of them dead.

"Yo, let's wrap this up. I got to make a move," Carter said, trying to cut the night short. He didn't feel comfortable around Murder and wanted him gone.

Zyir picked up on Carter's vibe and agreed. Mecca was slipping, and Carter was going to tell him about himself later.

The next day, Mecca had a talk with Carter, and he instantly cut off Murder. They also shut down that location as a drop-off and pick-up spot. Carter didn't know if Murder was a fed or an enemy, but he knew one thing: he could never be a part of The Cartel

Chapter Fifteen

"The Cartel runs this city, not y'all. You work for us!"
–Zyir

Breeze paced the spacious room back and forth, trying not to think about the subject that overwhelmed her thoughts. She was battling her conscience, and also the pain that was in the pit of her stomach. Heroin was calling for her, and she was on the brink of answering.

No, Breeze, you can't. I can fight this shit, she thought as she clutched her stomach and fell to her knees in pain. The pain that shot through her stomach was almost unbearable as she collapsed to all fours and began to cry.

Breeze couldn't understand what was going on with her body. She had never had an itch so bad, and whether she knew it or not, she was going through withdrawal. She was so used to getting dope shot into her veins on a daily basis that the first time her body went without it, it became excruciating. She kept thinking about what her father would say if he saw her in the state that she was in at that moment.

Breeze stood to her feet and took a deep breath while still clenching her stomach. She was ashamed of what she was about to do, but she couldn't help it. She had to shoot the magic into her veins immediately. She had to. She craved the warm sensation that the dope had when it crawled up her veins after injecting it. She kept thinking about how good it

would make her feel, and that thought alone was almost orgasmic. She had spent the last fifteen minutes going back and
forth, hoping that she would have enough willpower to fight
the urge. However, when that monkey is on a person's back,
all logic goes out the window.

Breeze quickly rushed to Zyir's room and began to search
through his drawers, trying to find any money she could. She
ran across a rubber band full of hundreds, and immediately
clipped two of the crisp bills. She then rushed to the front
room and grabbed Zyir's car keys. She was out the door and
on her way to the trap to cop a fix.

Breeze cruised the streets, searching for a dope boy to serve
her a fix. She had on a jogging suit with house shoes on her
feet as she pushed the new model Benz down the street. Before, she would never have been caught looking anything less
than glamorous, but now it was a different story. She was no
longer street royalty. She was just a junkie looking for a fix.
She was a completely different person than she once was, and
life had taken a toll on her.

She pulled onto a side street that was known for drug trafficking and parked her car. She noticed a group of young thugs posted
on a stoop and waved one of them over. All eyes were on Breeze
as she posted on the block and waited for the young hustler to
approach her car. Breeze was fidgety and anxious as she tapped
her wheel repeatedly, waiting for the guy to approach.

"What's up, ma?" the hustler asked as he bent his head down
and licked his lips.

"What's up? You got some 'boy'?" Breeze asked, cutting
straight to the point while clenching her stomach.

The young thug squinted his eyes and recognized Breeze
when he looked closer. He couldn't believe what she was ask-

ing him for. Here she was, the daughter of Carter Diamond, sister of the most ruthless gangster, and the dream girl for any dope boy that ever laid eyes on her, and she was looking to cop some dope from him. He instantly knew that she was craving dope from her body language.

"What?" he asked, thinking he had heard her wrong.

"You heard me. Do you got some or not?" she demanded again, but this time she pulled out a hundred dollar bill from her bra. The hustler couldn't believe what she was asking, and he knew that her brother would not appreciate him serving Breeze, so he stepped back and shook his head.

Breeze smacked her lips and put up her middle finger as she began to look past him, searching for a willing hustler.

"You know I can't do that. This is Mecca and Zyir's territory, ma. You can't do that," he said, trying to put her up on game without getting disrespectful. He knew that the dope he had in his pocket came from The Cartel, and to give it to Breeze would be straight up violating.

"Nigga, fuck what you talking about? You just scared, that's all," Breeze said as she waved him off, dismissing him like a flunky. At that point, she bruised the young hustler's ego, and it noticeably got to him.

"I'm not scared of yo' peoples, believe that. I just ain't for the bullshit that comes along with this," he responded.

"Like I said, you scared," Breeze said as she realized that her words were getting him upset. Breeze was smart enough to know that when a man's ego is bruised, it'll make him do things he usually would not do. In this case, he played right into Breeze's hand.

"Look, ma, I ain't scared of no damn body. I just—"

"You just a pussy," Breeze interrupted as she waved the hundred dollar bill in the air. The hustler looked around and then reached into the car, snatching the money out of

Breeze's hand. He then dug into his pocket and pulled out two packs of dope and tossed it on her lap.

"There you go. Fuck it," he said as he stood back up, feeling like a big man.

Breeze's eyes went directly to her lap and on the packs. Her eyes lit up and her anxiety went into overdrive as she anticipated what was to happen next. She couldn't wait to get back to Zyir's house. She wanted to shoot up immediately.

"Yo, is it somewhere I can take my medicine?" Breeze asked as she turned off the car and looked at the hustler.

"Yeah, up there," he said as he threw his head in the direction of the house behind him. "Just go through the back and then you can do your thing in there," he said, feeling like a big man now that he had served her.

Before he could complete his sentence, Breeze was out of the car and headed to the back of the house. All of the hustlers looked at her as she passed as if she were crazy. They looked at her nice body and the jogging pants that hugged her petite behind.

Breeze went to the back of the house and entered. The foul smell of blood and body odor filled the air as Breeze made her way through the shooting gallery, a nickname junkies gave a residence where users went to shoot their dope. Breeze walked through the house and saw different people scattered throughout the studio-style place, all using their preferred drug.

She stepped over a man that was laid out on the floor in a deep nod and found a table that was in the far corner. She quickly sat down and pulled out her two packs. She reached into her purse and got a shooter, also known as a syringe, and began to set up. Once she melted down the drug and got everything in order, she was ready to take the mystical train to cloud nine. As she filled the syringe with the smack, she felt her vagina get wet as if she were about to have sex with her dream man; however, the only thing that was about to go into her was a needle filled with heroin.

She pulled off the jacket to her jogging suit and grabbed a belt that someone had left on the table. She tied the belt around her arm and fastened it as tightly as she could. She put the end of the belt in between her teeth to keep the tension. She slowly pushed up the syringe to eject the water that was at the tip, and prepared to put it into the big green vein that had formed on her forearm. She slid the syringe into her vein and slowly ejected herself with the dope.

She instantly became relaxed, and a small smile formed on her face as her eyes closed. Drool began to creep out of the left side of her mouth as she slumped into the chair. Within seconds, she had slipped into a deep nod, and all her pain was temporarily taken away from her.

Unbeknownst to Breeze, another hustler by the name of Scoot had known about the relationship Zyir and Breeze once shared, and he immediately called his mentor to tell him that Breeze was inside of the dope house shooting up. Scoot knew that once Zyir or Mecca found out that Breeze had been served on one of The Cartel's blocks, it would be hell to pay. That's exactly why Scoot called Zyir to notify him, hoping he would be saving his own ass.

Zyir sped down the street with Illiana in the passenger's seat. Their lunch date was cut short by a phone call Zyir had received moments ago. "Can't believe this shit," Zyir whispered as he maneuvered through traffic, trying to get to Breeze. Illiana sat in the passenger's seat with her hands crossed over her chest tightly. She had a major attitude, and the way that Zyir cared for Breeze had her jealous.

"Just let her be," Illiana said as she rolled her eyes at Zyir. He shot a look over to Illiana that said much more than words could describe. Basically, if looks could kill, Illiana would have been dead right then and there.

Zyir pulled onto the block, turning the corner almost on two wheels. He stepped out of the car and began yelling. "Where she at?" he asked no one in particular.

Everyone pointed to the house, and Zyir quickly entered his dope house and scanned the room. What he saw in the corner broke his heart. Breeze was nodding, with a syringe stuck in her arm.

"No, Breeze . . . no," Zyir whispered as he slowly walked over to Breeze. She was so high she didn't even know that he was there. Zyir reached Breeze and dropped to his knees so he could be eye level with her. He slowly took the syringe out of her arm and forcefully threw it across the room in anger. He then grabbed Breeze by the face and lightly smacked her, trying to wake her up.

"Wake up, beautiful. It's time to go," he said as his heart ached. Seeing Breeze high was one of the worst things he could ever endure. He loved Breeze, and he refused to let her continue down the path of destruction.

"Breeze!" he called again.

"Hey, Zyir," she said in a slurred voice, barely opening her eyes. She smiled goofily because the drug had her in a total daze, and her body was completely relaxed.

"Come on, baby," he said as he picked her up and headed out the door. Zyir kissed Breeze on the forehead gently as she kept nodding uncontrollably.

"Open the door," he ordered to Illiana. She rolled her eyes and got out to do as he requested.

Zyir slid Breeze into the back seat and then closed the door. Zyir immediately pulled out his gun and made his way to the stoop where the hustlers were posted.

"Who served her?" Zyir asked with an ice-grill expression on his face. He was extremely upset, and was about to show the youngsters how The Cartel got down. "Who?" he asked again after not getting an immediate response. The hustlers on the stoop knew that Zyir meant business, so it did not take long for the finger pointing to begin. Zyir saw that everyone, including Scoot, pointed out the guy who had sold the dope to Breeze. Zyir instantly grabbed the dude by the neck and put the gun in his mouth.

"I want everybody to listen and listen close," Zyir yelled, trying to get everyone's attention. Everyone on the block looked at Zyir as he dragged the young hustler to the middle of the street. "Nobody serves Breeze. Do you fuckin' hear me? The Cartel runs this city, not y'all. You work for us!" he yelled, something that he rarely did. "If I hear about anybody giving her dope, this is what's going to happen."

Boom! A single shot rang through the air as the young hustler's brains were blown all over the pavement. His body instantly went limp and dropped. Zyir released his grip and let him fall.

The entire block was stunned. It was so quiet, you could hear a pin drop. Zyir had just shut down the whole block with a single shot. Zyir wiped the blood off of his face and looked around, giving every single hustler direct eye contact. He sent a message that would be embedded in each one of their hearts forever.

Zyir sat with Breeze twenty-four hours a day for weeks as she kicked her habit cold turkey. It was so painful for him to watch her body go through withdrawal, but he knew that it was for the best. By giving her tough love, he was saving her from herself. She had not asked to be introduced to addiction, but she was allowing it to eat her alive. He knew that she was strong enough to overcome the monkey on her back; all he had to do was convince her of that. He had never thought he would see the day that she would be so strung out, and he had to remind himself daily that she did not choose this lifestyle; it had been forced upon her.

The more time he put in with Breeze, the more irritated Illiana became. Zyir didn't have time to babysit her, however. His only focus was helping Breeze get better. He even missed out on money to be with her. Everything in his life was put on hold. Nothing mattered more than she did. This was not a battle that she could fight on her own, so he was going to walk with her and fight it for her every step of the way.

Nobody really understood the connection that he felt for her. All they saw was a black girl who had been lost to the game, but in her, Zyir saw so much more. He knew that the girl he loved was still somewhere inside of her. All he had to do was love her through her pain and help her get back to the beautiful young girl she used to be.

Breeze's body went through hell and back. Zyir saw things come out of her that no man ever wanted to see, but he never turned his back on her. There were even days when she degraded herself. She had been so used to being used and abused that she offered to trade sex for drugs with Zyir. She had no clue how her words tore his heart out of his chest. All she knew was that she wanted her fix.

Zyir attributed everything to the heroin and took it all in, absorbing the pain every day in order to help her get better. Zyir did not care for many people, but for Breeze he would go to the end of the world and back. She had captured his heart and loyalty forever. He knew that she would never be the perfect girl. She was too jaded, too scarred to revert back completely, but as long as she was able to get clean, she would be perfect for him. That's all that he could ask of her, and he was doing all in his power to ensure that she made it through.

Chapter Sixteen

"I'm the only fucking professional out of the bunch."
—Robyn

Carter sat at his dining table as he stared in disbelief at the information in front of him. After hiring a private investigator, he had found out Miamor's true profession. The truth was staring him in the face, and he finally understood why Mecca's hatred for Miamor ran so deep. A part of him wondered if what they had was even real.

He refused to believe that she was playing him just to get to The Cartel. He had gotten inside her head, he had explored the space between her legs, and had learned to control her heart. The way he had loved her was rare. He had never given himself to a woman the way he had with Miamor. To think that it was all a lie was unfathomable.

Before him were pictures of the Murder Mamas, newspaper clippings from the crimes they committed, and an address where they could be found now. Carter's P.I. had tracked them down in California. As the evidence of Miamor's ruthlessness haunted him, he felt an overwhelming urge to speak with the members of her crew who were still standing. He remembered meeting them once at the club, but had no idea how dangerous the ladies were at the time. As he found out about Miamor's life as a murderer for hire, he developed a newfound attraction to her. She was the best at what she did.

She could've trusted me with this secret, he thought.

The Murder Mamas' track record was so brutal that he knew he was lucky to be alive. Even none of his own young gunners had the body count that Miamor and her crew had attained.

If I had known, I would have put her down with The Cartel, he thought, impressed and intrigued all at the same time. Miamor had truly been one of a kind, and he did not know how much so until now.

Through all the anger and confusion he felt, the love he had for her was still present. Despite the fact that she had played a vital part in the demise of his family, the spell she had cast on him was still too potent for him to shake her loose. Her spirit was with him. He was in love with a killer—a Murder Mama.

They could have been the power couple sitting at the top if she had just been honest with him. Her hatred for his family could have been resolved, her ongoing beef with Mecca settled, if only she had told him the truth.

She was ruthless, but she had bitten off more than she could chew when she became Mecca's opposition, and as much as he wanted to, he could not blame Mecca for the decision he had made to put her down.

Carter finally understood that he was not the only one involved in a love affair with Miamor. Mecca had had his own relationship with her as well, but instead of exchanging whispers and kisses in the night, Mecca and Miamor exchanged hollow points and warfare. They had been enemies of the worst kind.

Mecca was right. Would she have killed me next? He had to know the answer, and the only way to find out was to talk to the people who had known her best.

He looked at the California address once more and hopped

up. He had to see Robyn and Aries. They were the ones who could give him the answers he so desperately sought.

Carter cocked his gun to load a single bullet in his semi-automatic and removed the safety as he placed it on his hip before getting out of the car. He carefully approached the front door to Robyn and Aries' place. Their good looks concealed their malicious intent, but now that Carter knew how they got down, he would not be caught slipping. He didn't come to play games; he simply wanted answers. A conversation was all he wanted, and he hoped that they could put aside their hatred for him for the moment.

He placed his hand near his waistline as he knocked on the door. When Aries pulled it open, she gasped in surprise. A mix of emotions filled her as she pulled her baby .380 without hesitation and pointed it directly in Carter's face.

"Aries, who is it?" Robyn shouted from the kitchen.

As tears filled Aries' eyes, she couldn't move her mouth to answer.

Carter didn't flinch as he stared at Aries sincerely. "I'm not here for all that. I come in peace. I just want to talk."

Aries' lip quivered as she thought of pulling the trigger on the man that Miamor had loved. "You let she die," Aries whispered.

"Aries! Who is it?" Robyn asked as she walked up and pulled the door open fully. She stopped and stared Carter in the eyes. "Shoot him," she said.

"Me friend is dead because of you," Aries said again.

"I know. Please, I just need to know more. I know about everything, about her affiliation with the Murder Mamas, and I just really need to speak with the two of you. I have to know if anything she said to me was ever real. Was I just a target?" Carter asked.

Both Aries and Robyn could see the pain in his eyes. Aries lowered her gun and stepped to the side as Robyn relieved him of his weapon.

"Are you alone?" Robyn asked reluctantly.

"Nobody knows that I'm here," he replied.

"Come in," she said as she led him to the kitchen table, while Aries walked behind him with her gun still in her hand.

Carter took a seat across from Aries as Robyn went back into the kitchen.

She emerged with two plates of food. "We were about to eat. You might as well join us." She placed the food in front of Aries and Carter before going to fix her own.

Once they were all comfortable at the table, Aries asked, "How did you find us?"

"If your money is long enough, anybody can be found," he replied.

"Well, you didn't come all the way out here for nothing, so what do you want to know?" Robyn asked.

"Was I just another target to Miamor?" Carter asked.

"Miamor wasn't a dumb girl. She stayed in Miami to be with you, not get at you. She loved you even though we told her she was crossing the line," Robyn admitted.

"Our target was The Cartel. Mia did not know chu were a part of it until she saw you at your brother's funeral. We came to shoot up the entire front row, but she called it off when she saw chu. We tried to get she to stop seeing you, Carter, but she wouldn't," Aries revealed.

His relief could be felt around the table as he sighed deeply. He had flown three thousand miles just to hear those words.

"She's dead because of you. If she had come here with us, she would still be alive. Her death is on you. I hope you know that," Robyn stated sadly.

"I think about it every day," he admitted.

"Thinking about it don't bring she back, Carter. What are chu going to do about it?" Aries asked. "We know who did this to she. Chu didn't know before, but now you can't play dumb. Chu know everything. Something has to be done."

Carter sat back in his chair. "He's my brother," Carter whispered in turmoil.

"Well, he isn't ours," Robyn stated harshly.

"No matter what happens from this point, she isn't coming back," Carter stated, heartbroken. "I loved Miamor. I had plans to have her in my life for a long time. I just want the two of you to know that. Nothing about what I felt for her was fake." Carter stood and Robyn handed him his gun back. "Thank you for telling me what I needed to know," he said.

"Chu are welcome," Aries stated.

Robyn walked him to the door and came back to find Aries reaching for Carter's plate of food.

Out of nowhere, she slapped the fork out of her hand, sending it flying clear across the room.

"Ow, bitch! What the fuck did chu do that for?" Aries asked, looking at Robyn as if she had lost her mind.

"Okay, go ahead and eat it. You know how I get down. I don't give a fuck if the nigga came over here to pour out his love for Miamor. You know what I put in that. The nigga was just too smart for his own damn good. He didn't even touch his plate," Robyn replied with a smirk.

Aries burst out laughing as she pushed the plate away. "Thanks for the heads up."

Robyn cracked up too and playfully answered, "With your friendly ass. I don't know what it is about that pretty-ass nigga. All my girls turn to mush around his ass. First Mia, now you! I swear I'm the only fucking professional out of the bunch."

Chapter Seventeen

"When the Mexicans come, they'll come with the army of an entire country behind them."
—*Carter*

Breeze was finally adjusting to being back home, and although weaning her body off of heroin was an everyday struggle, with the help of Zyir, she finally felt a sense of belonging again.

He was great for her in so many ways. Despite the time that had passed between them, they were able to pick up right where they left off. They were so close that it seemed as if they lived in a world by themselves. They rocked with one another and no one else. He was her best friend, and she loved him for not judging her.

She was still very rough around the edges. The glamour and prestige of the young, spoiled Breeze Diamond no longer existed. Now she was simple, timid, and trying to find her new identity as a young woman who had lived a rough life. She had seen too many bad things to go back to the naïve princess she had once been. Life had grown her up, and now Zyir was helping to stabilize her.

Most of her family was dead. The only people that she had left were her two brothers and Zyir. Those relationships meant everything to her. They were the only normalcy she knew, and everyone else was considered an outsider.

As she lay in bed, Zyir knocked on the door and peeked his head inside.

"You awake, ma?" he asked.

Breeze sat up against the headboard and smiled as she fixed her frazzled ponytail. She patted the bed beside her, motioning for him to sit next to her.

"Yeah, I'm up," she replied as he crawled into her bed. He kissed her cheek.

"You good?" he asked. "You need anything?"

Breeze shook her head and replied, "Just you, Zyir. You're so good to me. I don't know what I would do without you."

"You don't have to think about that, Breeze. You will never have to be without me. I'ma always be here for you," he whispered.

Breeze shook her head and replied, "How long do you think your little girlfriend is going to let me stick around? She don't want me here, Zyir. You say you will be here now, but when she makes you choose . . ."

"I'ma choose you," he replied. "You know me, ma. I'm not into knockoffs. I need the real thing, and now that you're back, it's a wrap for everyone else."

Breeze blushed as she lowered her chin to her chest. "Compared to Illiana I'm the knockoff. She's beautiful, Zyir. I can't compete with that . . . not anymore."

Zyir could hear the insecurity in her voice, and it bruised him deeply because no other woman could hold a candle to Breeze. She was in a league all her own. She used to know this, but her self-esteem had been beaten into the ground, and now she felt threatened.

He had already stopped sleeping with Illiana. Out of respect for Breeze, he slept on the couch, but he could see that the better Breeze's health became, the more she felt second rate to Illiana. Balancing the personalities of the two women was hard for Zyir, and although he wanted to cut Illiana off completely, he knew that he would have to do it slowly. The last thing he wanted to do was create a riff between the Garza Cartel and Carter's operation, because he had made the mistake of becoming sexual with Illiana.

"You don't have to compete, Breeze. She doesn't mean anything to me. I'm only worried about you right now," he said. "Okay?"

She nodded her head. "Okay."

"I know what you need, ma. You need to get out of the house. Is shopping still your favorite pastime?" he asked playfully.

"I haven't been in so long I might not remember how to do it," she replied with a laugh.

Zyir reached into his pocket and began to pull out a knot of cash, but he stopped himself. He didn't want to put any money in Breeze's hand. Although she had shaken off her addiction, her sobriety was important to Zyir, and he did not think she was ready to have cash in her hands.

It might be too much temptation for her, he thought.

"I'm going to arrange for a driver to take you and Illiana shopping today. I'll leave some money with her, and you can go relax. Enjoy a day out on me. The sky is the limit, so get whatever you want," he said.

Breeze nodded and closed her eyes as Zyir kissed her forehead before walking out of the room.

The limousine was silent as Illiana and Breeze were escorted to Bal Harbour's elite shopping boutiques. It was obvious that the girls did not care for one another. Their only connection was Zyir, and each felt like her position in his life was threatened as long as the other was around.

Illiana sipped on champagne as she looked Breeze up and down from behind the tint of her Chanel shades. As the limo pulled curbside, Illiana stepped out of the car and did not wait for Breeze before she strutted into the boutique. Expecting to be catered to, she was taken aback when the salespeople bypassed her to service Breeze. The Diamond family's legacy was known throughout the city, and as much as Breeze used to frequent the shops, her face had not been forgotten. The salespeople waited on her hand and foot, while Illiana shopped alone, heeated.

Breeze was overwhelmed by all of the attention, but it felt good to knock Illiana off of her high horse. For the first time since her return, she was receiving the type of respect that her last name demanded, and it felt good. She could feel Illiana's envy all the way across the room. Soon Breeze was back in her element, and she found herself buying up everything in sight as she went from designer shop to designer shop. Before she knew it, the day had passed by and they were back in the limousine headed home.

Illiana was steaming, and she was determined to knock Breeze off of her high horse. She rolled down the window that separated them from the driver and said, "I need to make a detour to Sixty-third Street." She was about to take Breeze to the infamous Pork 'n Beans Projects in Liberty City. Tired of playing nice, Illiana had something sinister in store for Breeze that would be sure to banish her from Zyir's life forever.

The luxury Chrysler limousine seemed out of place in the dilapidated housing community, and the weary corner boys looked on curiously as it rolled to a stop.

"What are we doing here?" Breeze asked Illiana as she peered out of the tinted windows.

"I just need to cop a little something to take the edge off," Illiana replied devilishly as she saw a familiar spark go off inside of Breeze. "You need anything, or you good?"

Breeze shook her head as she felt the familiar tingle of anticipation fill her loins. All of a sudden, her craving came back full force. "No, I . . . I'm good," she replied.

Illiana shrugged her shoulders and got out of the car, taking only a hundred dollar bill with her. She quickly copped Breeze's drug of choice and hurried back to the limo.

"I got you a little something just in case," Illiana said as soon as she stepped back inside. She opened her hand to reveal the tiny packs of dope that she had inside. Breeze's eyes widened eagerly as she reached out her hand to grab them, but she resisted and snatched her hand back as if it were on fire.

"I can't. I promised him," Breeze said as she tried to convince herself to do the right thing.

"Who said anybody besides you and me has to know?" Illiana replied. Breeze didn't respond, but Illiana already knew that Breeze was going to indulge.

Once a junkie, always a junkie, Illiana thought. She placed the packs on the seat beside Breeze and watched in amusement as Breeze slowly but surely picked them up and tucked them inside her jean pocket.

She could not wait to get back to Zyir's place and get high. She was so anxious that she began to fidget in her seat.

Illiana had just sent Breeze spiraling back down into the abyss, hindering her recovery. There was no remorse to be felt by her, however. Life was a game of chess, not checkers, and Illiana didn't care how many queens she had to destroy in order to win.

Zyir walked into his place, exhausted from a long day of hustling. His home was unusually quiet, and an eerie feeling passed over him as he entered. It was two A.M., and he knew that Breeze and Illiana were probably asleep. He knocked on the guest bedroom door. He didn't want to disturb her, but he had to see her face before he went to bed. Ever since Breeze had been back, seeing her face had been like a blessing to him. Her smile made him smile, and he wanted to see how her day had gone before he retired for the night.

When she didn't respond, he opened the door and eased inside. Her bed was perfectly made, and he frowned when he saw her sitting on the floor in the dark with her back leaned lazily against the bed.

"B, you a'ight in here?" he asked as he stepped inside.

He turned on the light, and what he saw enraged him. Breeze was on the floor, in a deep nod, as drool ran out of the side of her lip. The belt she had used to produce a vein was still tied around her arm, and the empty packs of heroin littered the bedroom floor.

Zyir bit into his bottom lip to stop himself from screaming out loud as he rushed over to her side. "I told them niggas. I told 'em," he mumbled as he saw red. The burner on his hip was calling his name. There was no doubt that he was going to murder a nigga tonight.

"Breeze, wake up, ma. Wake up," he said as he picked up her frail body from the floor. "Breeze!" he shouted as he slapped her face gently to stir her from the nod.

He carried her wildly into the adjoining bathroom as he placed her in the bathtub and turned on the shower. The shock of the cold water woke her up.

"You promised me, ma," he said in defeat as he got on his knees to stare her in the eyes. He gripped the sides of her head tightly. He was so angry with her, so disappointed in her. "You were doing so good. Fuck was you thinking, Breeze?" he shouted.

"I'm sorry," she replied, her eyelids still low. "I can't stop."

"Who gave you this shit?" Zyir screamed like a maniac. He

was so livid that he thought about striking her, but he could not bring himself to do it.

She can't help it. It's not her fault, he kept telling himself.

"Who served you?" he asked.

A slight smile spread across her lips as Breeze whispered, "Your fucking girlfriend did, okay! I was trying, but I'm not strong enough to kick this, Zyir. Illiana gave it to me. I could have said no, but I took it. I wanted it."

Before Breeze could finish her sentence, Zyir was up and out of the room with a flash. He was so out of his mind that he didn't stop to think before he burst into his bedroom. A sleeping Illiana was caught by surprise when Zyir pulled her out of his bed by her legs.

"Bitch, you gave that shit to her?" he asked. Not waiting for an answer, he smacked fire from Illiana.

"No! Zyir, she's lying!" Illiana screamed as Zyir's open hand closed and came barreling across her face. She saw stars as he attacked her relentlessly. "No! Please stop!" she hollered, but the soundproof walls intercepted all of her pleas. She had no choice but to take this ass-whooping.

Zyir went bananas on Illiana. Beating a woman was so out of his character, but he had snapped. All he could see was an addicted Breeze as he punished Illiana.

She curled up in a fetal position and tried to cover her face as Zyir loomed over her, raining punches down over her.

"You dirty bitch," Zyir raged. He straddled her and wrapped his hands around her neck as he squeezed the life out of her. Zyir didn't come back to reality until he felt someone's hands pulling him off of her. He heard Breeze sobbing by the doorway.

"Zyir!" Carter yelled as he hemmed him up. "Chill out!"

Sweating profusely and breathing erratically, Zyir was an emotional mess.

"Is she dead?" he asked as his rage subsided. He noticed that Illiana wasn't moving. "Fuck!" he yelled.

Carter kneeled over her still body to check her pulse and answered, "She's alive, but I've got to get her to a doctor. This is bad, Zyir. You know who she's connected to. Fuck was you thinking?" Carter knew that if Breeze had not called him, then Zyir probably would have killed Illiana.

"I wasn't. She gave Breeze dope and I lost it!" he whispered as he looked back at a fearful Breeze. He quickly turned his head. He couldn't even look at her right now.

"You know what this means, right?" Carter asked.

Zyir nodded. "I'm sorry, bro. I spazzed." Wearing his heart on his sleeve was so uncharacteristic for Zyir, but Breeze was his weak spot. Ever since she came home, he had been a loose cannon, acting without thinking about the repercussions.

"As long as you're prepared to deal with the consequences. This is the beginning of another war, and this time, we can't afford to lose."

"What about her? What are we going to do about her?" Zyir asked.

"I'm going to get her admitted into the hospital. When she wakes up, she'll call for her family without a doubt. We just have to be prepared, because when the Mexicans come, they'll come with the army of an entire country behind them.

Chapter Eighteen

"Don't know, but I'm ready for whatever."
—Zyir

Murder forcefully flipped down his phone after he got a disconnection message when he tried to call Mecca. He knew something was up because Mecca had gotten his number changed and hadn't called him back. Murder kept regretting the fact that he had Carter, Zyir, and Mecca in a room all together and didn't pop off.

"Damn it!" Murder yelled as he began to pace the room. He was determined to kill The Cartel. He was done playing around and trying to sneak his way in. He was about to blow heads off and play it how it went.

Murder loaded up some explosives that he had purchased from one of Aries and Robyn's weapons connect. He gently paced them in a duffel bag and prepared to take them to the warehouse that Mecca had taken him to. He knew eventually that they would meet there again, and when that time came, he was going to light that warehouse up like the Fourth of July. Murder loaded up and headed out, seeking blood.

Carter and Zyir made it to the hotel where Breeze and Mecca were staying. They were about to have a small meeting and decide on what to do about the new problem with the Garza Cartel.

Carter had switched cars, and his paranoia was at an all-time high. He knew that his team was no match for Felipe and his organization. Felipe had a whole country behind him, so no matter how many goons Carter killed, Felipe would just keep sending crews until The Cartel was completely dead.

Carter tried to call Mecca, but his phone kept going straight to voice mail. Carter noticed when he was pulling up to the hotel's entrance that the door was blocked off and an UNDER CONSTRUCTION sign was put up.

"We probably have to go through the back," Zyir said as he took a look at the blocked off door.

It was something like no other. Twenty-two bodies lay sprawled out on the block at 10 o'clock in the morning. The same block where Zyir had blown off the hustler's head now looked like a battleground after combat. All of the hustlers and some of the drug users were dead at the hands of automatic assault rifles. More than five hundred shell casings were scattered over the block, and the Garza Cartel was the cause of this melee.

Felipe had declared war and sent his hoodlums to kill anything moving. Anyone who had anything to do with The Cartel was a target. It was something that Miami had never seen before, and it was only the beginning.

Illiana failed to mention to Felipe that she had slipped Breeze dope, and only told her family about the beating Zyir had put on her. Needless to say, they were infuriated. The sad part was that this was only the beginning.

Zyir and Carter pulled onto the block to witness the scene. Carter shook his head from side to side as he thought about what Zyir had gotten them into. Carter couldn't get too mad, because he knew that he would have reacted the same way if he had caught Illiana giving Breeze the dope.

"This isn't good," Carter said in a low tone as he slowly drove by the scene, not wanting to stop. Zyir looked at the bodies and saw his li'l man Scoot lying awkwardly on the pavement with blooding leaking from his body.

"Damn, the kid was only sixteen years old," Zyir said as he quickly turned his head, trying to look at the kid's lifeless eyes.

Police had begun to rope off the area, and ambulances were at the scene, but it was all for nothing, because there was no one to save. Everyone was dead.

Just as Carter reached the end of the block, they were taken by surprise. Two white vans without windows blocked Carter's car, boxing him in so he couldn't escape.

"What the fuck?" Carter said under his breath as he watched the scene unfold. He didn't realize what was going on, but he would soon find out. A third van quickly pulled up in front of Carter's car, and the sliding doors on all the vans seemed to open at the same time.

Three men jumped out of each van, all of them carrying military assault rifles. They began to riddle the car with bullets. The Garza Cartel had orchestrated a perfect hit. They knew that Carter, Zyir, or Mecca would visit the crime scene, and preyed in anticipation until they eventually showed up.

Carter quickly ducked down, and Zyir did also. The thuds of the bullets hitting the car sounded like a hailstorm, as the gunmen spared no ammunition and lit the car up in broad daylight.

Luckily, Carter was driving his bulletproof Benz, and no bullets penetrated the interior of his car.

The Miami police ducked for cover and began to call for backup on their walkie-talkies as the block underwent pandemonium. Some of the officers began to run toward the gunmen with their guns drawn, demanding them to drop their weapons. The Mexicans didn't care if they were uniformed cops. They shot at them also. In their country, there was no authority above their cartel. The Mexican gunplay was too much for the officers, and the Miami Police Department had to back down and wait for help.

After noticing that Carter's car was bulletproof, one of the gunmen said something in Spanish, and the Mexicans hopped in their vans and peeled off, leaving black tire marks on the pavement and smoking tires. Carter and Zyir grabbed their guns from under the seat and watched as the vans disappeared off the block. Both of their hearts were pounding rapidly as they escaped the deadly ambush by the skin of their teeth.

"You good?" Carter asked as he looked Zyir's body up and down to see if he was hit.

"Yeah, I'm good. You?" Zyir asked as he breathed heavily.

"Yeah," Carter responded as his phone began to ring. He looked at the caller ID and noticed that the incoming call was blocked. Carter picked up the phone and heard the operator's voice. The call was from a federal penitentiary.

"I accept," Carter spoke into the phone.

"My dear friend, I am hurt that you crossed the line . . . and for that, you will suffer," Garza said calmly and confidently. "I have no control over what happens after this point. My only advice to you is to flee as far away as you can. There is nowhere in the country where Felipe can't find you and your family. With that, I'll say good-bye," Garza said just before hanging up the phone.

Carter didn't know what to say, so he didn't say anything. He just closed his phone and shook his head from side to side.

"We have to get out of here," Carter said as he steered the bullet-riddled car off the block. The tires were flattened, but Carter wanted to leave before the cops approached them, asking questions.

Zyir and Carter were silent because they knew that they had just started a war with one of the deadliest cartels in North America.

In the meantime, Breeze was asleep in a hotel room, with Mecca present with her. Mecca was up looking out of the window with a gun in his hand. After giving him the news of the melee on their block, Carter had told him to check into a hotel downtown just to be safe. He knew that Illiana knew about their personal residences, and he didn't want to take any chances.

Mecca looked at the gun in his hand and shook his head. He didn't feel the same adrenaline rush that he once did when feeling the cold steel in his palms. Actually, it started to disgust him. Mecca was tired of selling drugs, tired of murders, and tired of The Cartel. He knew that if his family wasn't a part of The Cartel, they would all be there with him and not dead.

He looked over at his sleeping beauty, his baby sister, and wanted more for her. He refused to lose her again.

Mecca's mind ran wild as he began to think about religion, and it seemed as if every time he closed his eyes, he saw a person's face that he had once murdered. Throughout his killing career, it never bothered him to look into the eyes of a person he killed, but now, it was crashing down on him like a ton of bricks.

Since Mecca was a young boy, he'd always wanted to be a gangster—nothing more, nothing less. But now he wanted to be just a regular man, a family man. His mind was clear since he hadn't been using drugs or drinking, and he really wanted a change.

This new beef with the Mexicans was one that Mecca didn't want to see. He knew the ramifications of a war, and he wasn't willing to lose any more family over it. Mecca glanced at Breeze once again and then walked over to her and knelt beside the bed next to her. He did something that he had not done since he was a little boy. He began to pray.

Carter and Zyir entered the hotel from the back entrance, using the keycard that was provided for the guests. They stepped in and saw three Mexican men run by them with guns in their hands. Carter and Zyir quickly ducked back and out of sight as the men whizzed by them, not even noticing them.

"What the fuck?" Zyir whispered as he and Carter pulled out their guns. Carter had underestimated the Garza Cartel. He knew that they had come for blood.

"Breeze and Mecca are up there!" Carter said as he looked around the corner and saw that the three Mexicans were headed up the stairs.

"Let's use the elevator," Carter suggested as he cocked back his gun and flipped it off safety. Zyir and Carter flew to the elevator, hoping that they would reach the fifth floor before the Mexican goons did.

Carter hurriedly tapped the button in the elevator, trying to make the doors close faster, and Zyir immediately hit the camera that was in the top corner of the elevator, knowing that they were about to get into some shit. The door finally closed and they began to go up.

"Come on, come on, come on," Zyir repeated as he stared at the numbers indicating what floor they were passing. They knew that they only had a small window of time to make it to the room before the Mexicans did.

"I wonder how many are here," Carter said, believing that Felipe had sent more than three men to do the job.

"Don't know, but I'm ready for whatever," Zyir said bravely

as he thought about his love, Breeze, who was in the room with Mecca.

They finally reached the fifth floor and—

"Where is the food?" Mecca asked, flicking through the channels as Breeze sat next to him in the bed.

"Just call Carter and tell him to bring us something on his way here," Breeze said, not wanting to eat the nasty hotel food anyway.

"Cool," Mecca agreed as he picked up his phone. "Damn, I don't have any service."

As soon as the words escaped his mouth, a knock on the door sounded.

"Room service," a maid announced with a heavy Spanish accent.

"Thank God! Finally some food," Breeze said as she sat upright and looked at the door.

Mecca got up and grabbed his pistol off of the bed, wanting to be cautious as he approached the door. He peeked through the peephole and was at ease when he saw that it was a maid with a platter in her hand. Mecca tucked his gun in his waistline and removed the chain lock that was on the door. He reached into his pocket and grabbed some money and opened the door.

As soon as the door opened, a Mexican man stepped into view with a sawed-off shotgun aimed directly at Mecca's chest. Before Mecca could even react, the loud sound of the shotgun rang through the air. The blast struck Mecca in his sternum, causing him to fly back viciously.

Breeze was startled by the blast, and she screamed at the top of her lungs as she saw her brother get blown off of his feet.

Breeze screamed at the top of her lungs as she tried to

scramble off of the bed and run for cover. The man ran in and grabbed Breeze by the hair and flung her violently across the room. He was speaking Spanish, so Breeze couldn't understand him, but his body language and facial expression clearly stated that he hated her and wanted her dead.

He grabbed her by the throat, still speaking Spanish, and he sinisterly smirked as he put the gun to Breeze's face. Boom! A loud shot rang throughout the hotel room, and blood and guts splattered all over Breeze's face—but not blood of her own. It was the blood of the gunman.

She screamed hysterically as the man lay slumped on her with his face blown off. Mecca stood behind him with a smoking gun. He ripped open his shirt, revealing his bulletproof vest, something he never left home without.

He pushed the man off of Breeze and helped her up.

"Are you okay?" he asked as he held his chest. It was tender, sore, and felt like it had been hit with a bat swung by Barry Bonds.

"Yeah, I'm good," Breeze answered as she hugged her brother tightly.

Mecca heard commotion in the hall and knew that there were more goons coming. He thought quickly and looked toward the window for an escape route.

"Come on," he said as he pulled Breeze toward the window, knowing that his one gun couldn't go up against whatever was about to come his way. Mecca, all of a sudden, heard shots ringing out and three bodies dropped, tumbling over one another. Mecca quickly pointed his gun at the door, ready to bust at whatever came through. He breathed heavily and stood in front of Breeze, willing to be her shield.

Carter and Zyir had just dropped the three Mexicans with their accurate shots, and they made their way to the room where they knew Mecca and Breeze were.

"Mecca!" Carter yelled as he ran down the hall with his gun in a firing position.

"In here!" he heard Mecca yell from the suite.

Zyir and Carter ran to the door, but looked back and noticed about ten more Mexicans coming from the staircase. Zyir and Carter quickly dipped into the room and closed the door, knowing that they only had seconds to think of something.

"Is Breeze okay?" Zyir asked as he ran to her and she hugged him tightly while still crying hysterically. "I got you, ma," Zyir whispered in her ear as he rubbed her hair. That moment was short-lived because Zyir knew that they would be busting in at any moment.

"How many?" Mecca yelled as he pointed his gun at the door along with Carter, waiting for them to come in.

"Too many," Zyir said as he shook his head.

"He's right. We can't win," Carter said as he thought about how many goons he saw at the far end of the hall, heading their way.

"We have to jump. It's the only way to make it out alive," Zyir said as he slid the patio door open and looked down at the pool five stories below.

"Fuck we waiting for?" Mecca asked frantically while still aiming at the door.

The sounds of bullets trying to shoot the lock off erupted, and they had to make their decision quick. The old Mecca would have never thought twice about shooting it out with the Mexicans and dying in the blaze of glory, but the new Mecca wanted to live. He thought about Leena and his nephew and the fact that he hadn't gotten his redemption yet. That reason alone was enough for him to concede defeat and try to escape.

"Fuck it!" Mecca said as he hurried to the balcony and looked over. Without hesitation, he jumped feet first into the deep pool. Breeze, then Zyir, followed suit and jumped also. Carter was the last to jump. Just before Carter jumped, the door flew open and the sounds of the drums letting loose and releasing numerous bullets sounded. Bullets whizzed by Carter's head and body, forcing him to jump prematurely. He landed into the water and they barely got away.

The Garza Cartel was too much for them to handle. Ruthless would have been an understatement.

Carter and Breeze were stationed outside of the warehouse, waiting for Zyir and Mecca to return. The plan was for them to retrieve all of their owed money out of the streets and flee the state. The long arm of the Garza Cartel was too much for Carter and The Cartel. Carter made an executive decision to leave town; he chose not to fight another war. He was smart enough to know when he could not win. The Cartel was not as strong as it once was, and this was the proof. The Mexicans had pushed them into a corner, and this was the last resort.

"Is everything going to be okay?" Breeze asked her big brother in her most innocent voice. Carter could sense the fear in her tone, and he calmly looked over at her and smiled.

"I got you, Breeze. Everything is going to be all right. Tonight is the last night we ever will step foot in Miami. This drug game has tore this family apart. I'm going to make sure that I put this family back together and start a new type of legacy, one built on love and not power. I got you, baby girl," he said as he leaned over and kissed her forehead.

Breeze felt warm inside, and for a brief second, she thought she was listening to her father. Young Carter resembled him so much, and he also had a way of letting her know that everything would be okay, just as her deceased father did when he was still alive. Breeze smiled and sat back in the seat, confident in his words.

"We just have to go in here, count the money, and wait for the sun to rise so we can head out to the airport," Carter said. He felt safe at the warehouse, knowing it was a spot that the Mexicans would not think to look for them. His plans were to end The Cartel's legacy that night and leave the drug game behind.

Mecca and Zyir pulled up with three duffel bags full of money. They had collected all of their funds out of the streets, and if blocks were short, they just took what they had and called it even. They needed cold, hard cash to relocate and start over.

Carter and Breeze saw Mecca's car pull behind them, and they got out of the car to enter the warehouse. Soon, they would all be on a private jet to an unknown location. Well, at least that was their plan.

Members of the Garza Cartel were parked about a half-mile away from the warehouse, waiting for The Cartel to arrive, and just as they thought, they were there. They were waiting for them to enter so they could go in and ambush them and leave them all dead. They looked through binoculars, watching the whole scenario unfold. Little did they know, they weren't the only eyes watching The Cartel on that night.

Murder waited patiently on the side of the building watching The Cartel walk in. He smiled as he thought about what was about to happen. He held a detonator in his lap. He was about to send all of them to hell, first class. Murder was doing this for Miamor, and it made him feel good inside.

He watched closely as they all entered the building just before he pulled away. He waited until he got far enough to be clear of the upcoming explosion.

"Fuck The Cartel," he mumbled as he pushed the button and heard the loud boom of the explosives go off. He began to drive away as the debris flew into the air and a massive fireball formed fifty feet into the air. His mission was done and The Cartel was officially over.

"May they all burn in hell," he said as he chuckled to himself, disappearing into the night.

The Last Chapter

"She probably is in hell, smoking a blunt. That's a real bitch."
—*Unknown*

"We are gathered here today to celebrate the lives of three of God's children."

The preacher stood before the many people who attended the funeral of street royalty. It was a sad day in Miami, and on this day, the streets were like a ghost town. It seemed as if the entire underworld had stopped to commemorate those they had lost. Everyone within the city limits felt this grief. The lives of three street legends had been destroyed, and grief overflowed in the ceremony as three silver-plated coffins sat side by side with an array of flower arrangements around them. It was a bright, sunny day, and it seemed as if God shone his light down from the heavens above to make that hard day seem a tad bit better for the mourning attendees. It was a triple funeral to bury the last of the Diamond family— Breeze, Carter, and Mecca.

The Cartel was no more, and it was the last chapter to what was to be named one of the biggest legacies in Miami's underworld history. Their story was legendary, ruthless . . . and most of all, classic.

Many people were in attendance, but the most important guests were not there to pay their final respects, but to confirm that the last of The Cartel was deceased and about to be buried into the ground.

Robin and Aries were in attendance, draped in all black dresses with big shades on to keep a low profile. Murder also sat beside them. The demise of The Cartel was bittersweet for him, and he gritted his teeth tightly as he thought about Mecca and the missed opportunity to personally kill him on Miamor's behalf. Nevertheless, Mecca was dead, and that would have to be enough for him.

Emilio Estes, Leena, and Monroe Jr. were also in attendance, mourning the loss. They were the only people left alive who could sit in the front pew reserved for family. Although far removed from the Diamond legacy, they were the last of a dying bloodline.

There was an eerie feeling in the air and everyone there could sense it. As the preacher held the Holy Bible tightly in his hand and read from the book of Psalms, a stretch limo with tinted windows rolled up slowly about fifty yards away from the service. Many people didn't notice it, but the trained eyes were glued to the approaching vehicle.

Emilio Estes looked back and saw the limo pull up, and he watched as it came to a slow stop. Estes knew exactly who it was; it was the crew responsible for the very funeral he was at. Emilio, being in his mid-sixties and not willing to step back into the streets, conceded defeat and pulled his white handkerchief from the top pocket of his suit.

To many, it looked as if Emilio was just removing a hanky, but veterans of the street game knew what that small gesture meant. Emilio wanted the bloodshed to stop, and signaled that he would not retaliate. The war was finally over and The Cartel was no more. Literally, he was waving a white flag. It was officially The Cartel's last chapter.

***

Breeze, Zyir, Mecca, and Carter were behind the tint of the stretch limo, watching their own funeral service. They had faked their own deaths, knowing that the Garza Cartel was too much for them. Carter knew that his suspicions about Murder were correct, and he had one of his goons trail Murder. He eventually found out that Murder had placed bombs at the warehouse. Carter then used that to his advantage. It was a risky plan, but it worked. As far as the Mexican beef, it was a war that they could never win so they outsmarted their enemy, rather than outshooting them. Carter came up with the plan to fake their deaths, and it worked like a charm.

Carter knew that the Garza Cartel would be watching them when they went to the warehouse, so he orchestrated a plan to sneak out of the back just before he blew the place up. He paid a coroner for four dead bodies that matched closely to himself, Zyir, Mecca, and Breeze, and placed them at the scene to be found by the authorities.

His plan had worked perfectly. They all sat in the limo with champagne glasses, celebrating their victory.

"This is to new beginnings. The Cartel is no more," Breeze said as she raised her glass. Everyone joined her as she began her toast. With the support of her family, she was doing so much better. She had vowed to never touch another drug in her life, and so far, she was beating her addiction. She was more than ready to leave everything behind.

"To The Car—" Mecca started. He forgot that The Cartel was news of the past. "My fault. That gangster shit still in me," he said while smiling. "To family," he said as he raised his glass a tad bit higher.

"To family," everyone said in unison, repeating what Mecca had just said. Another limo pulled up behind them, and they all knew that it was Felipe and his people. They had come to confirm their deaths.

Carter laughed and signaled for the driver to pull off. They had to catch a flight to Brazil. The Cartel was officially dead to the world.

2 Weeks Later in Brazil

Zyir looked at Breeze as she approached him with a flowing white dress and a veil over her face. Breeze had never looked more beautiful to him than she did on that very day.

Mecca walked on her right side, where their father should have been, and he gripped her hand for support. It was her wedding day, a day that their mother and father had looked forward to since Breeze was a young girl. Although they could not be present, Mecca felt their spirits in the air.

"They're looking down on you today, Breeze. They're here," Mecca whispered.

Breeze knew that he was speaking of their parents, and smiled as her eyes lifted to the sky to acknowledge them.

Carter was next to Zyir, acting as his best man for the ceremony. The only witness present outside of The Cartel family was the Catholic priest of the church they used.

Zyir smiled from ear to ear as he patiently waited to be joined by his bride. As they approached, Zyir looked at Breeze and promised himself that he would take care of her forever and a day. She made him happy, and he was determined to return that favor for a lifetime.

Zyir asked Breeze to marry him while they were on the jet coming to Brazil, and she graciously accepted. It didn't take long for them to start planning for the small ceremony and make it happen.

Breeze approached Zyir ,and they stood face to face, looking into each other's eyes.

Breeze was full of tears because not only was she overwhelmed with happiness, but also great sadness. She wanted to share this special day with her family, but she only had a few people left. This day had brought about mixed emotions for her. She had never missed her parents and Monroe more than she had today, but the man who stood before her gave her strength. In his eyes, she saw her future, and it was filled with love. Her newfound joy with Zyir allowed her to push the sadness out of her mind, and she smiled from ear to ear.

The priest began the ceremony, and it was nothing but love in the room. They were a match made in heaven.

"I now pronounce you man and wife. You may kiss the bride," the priest said as he smiled and nodded his head at Zyir.

Zyir then slowly raised the veil that covered Breeze's face and exposed her magnificence. He put both of his hands under her chin and kissed her.

Carter and Mecca clapped as Zyir kissed his wife. They both turned toward the door and started to walk down the aisle, but before Zyir took two steps, he turned back to Carter and whispered something that was one of the hardest things he ever had to ask him.

"Do you want me to take care of it?" Zyir asked.

Carter watched as Breeze hugged Mecca and looked at Zyir.

"Nah, I got it. Enjoy your wedding day. I will see you when you get back," he said calmly and smoothly, all with a small smile on his face. "I love you, Zy, Carter said to his protégé that was now a man.

"I love you too, big homie," Zyir replied.

***

Breeze approached Mecca as he held his arms out. He had tears in his eyes. Crying was something Breeze never saw Mecca do.

The tears in Mecca's eyes were ones of joy rather than pain. It felt good to see his sister smiling for a change. He saw that Zyir made her happy, and that was what was important to him.

He glanced at Zyir, who was talking to Carter, and smirked, knowing that Zyir would take good care of his sister. Mecca then focused back on the approaching Breeze.

"I love you, sis," Mecca said as she slid into his arms and into his warm embrace. Mecca was so happy to see his sister in the pretty white dress, and he knew that his mother and father would have been proud of her if they were still alive.

Their family had been through war and rain, but now it was time for sunshine. He was her only remaining full-blooded relative, and he knew that he symbolized more than himself. He was there on the behalf of Monroe, Taryn, and their father, Big Carter.

"I love you too, Mecca," Breeze said as she rested her head on his chest and hugged him tightly. Her eyes were closed, but a tear managed to slip down her cheek. She enjoyed that moment like it would be her last. The drama and turmoil that she had been through over the years with the ills of the drug game and the family business had her jaded.

She thought about being in the basement of Ma'tee's home and being hopeless and ready to die. She thought she would never escape his grasp, but to be married and starting a new chapter in her life brought joy to her heart.

Mecca wanted to confess to his sister and tell her all of the wrong he had done, just as he had done with the priest, but he could not bring himself to let Breeze know that he had betrayed the family in such a heinous way. How was he supposed to tell her that he had murdered his own twin brother and reignited the beef with the Haitians? All of Mecca's betrayals eventually led to the death of Taryn and Breeze's own kidnapping. How could he tell her this? He couldn't, because he feared that she would never forgive him, and he needed his sister to look at him with admiration as she had always done.

He needed her love like he needed the air in his lungs, so as he stood before her, the only words he could let slip out of his quivering lips were, "Sorry. I'm so sorry." He gently grabbed her shoulders and looked into her beautiful eyes. He saw his father's features in Breeze, and also their mother's, and it tore Mecca's insides apart.

Breeze looked into Mecca's eyes and felt his pain through the windows to his soul. She didn't understand fully what Mecca was sorry for, but something told her not to ask. Breeze just smiled and nodded her head.

"It's okay, Mecca. I forgive you," she whispered as she wiped the single tear that streamed down his clenched jawbone. She didn't know what she was forgiving Mecca for, but she understood that he needed to experience forgiveness. She felt obligated to let him know that whatever he had done, it was in the past.

Zyir finished his brief conversation with Carter and headed over to Mecca and Breeze. He approached Mecca as Breeze stepped back and gave them room to converse.

"Congratulations," Mecca whispered as he looked at his comrade, Zyir.

"Thanks, fam," Zyir said with a smirk on his face. He embraced Mecca and hugged him tightly as he cherished the moment. He knew Mecca was a gangster, and real always recognized real. Needless to say, Zyir respected Mecca and vice versa.

Mecca noticed that Zyir hugged him tightly, and Mecca felt the genuine love coming from his new brother-in-law. The moment was almost enough to make Mecca cry again, but he held his composure and respected the authenticity of Zyir.

Zyir hugged Mecca like it would be the last time he would see him. "I love you bro," Zyir said as he released his embrace.

"I love you too. Take care of my sister, a'ight," Mecca said as he winked at Breeze.

"I got you," Zyir said as he held out his arm for Breeze to latch on. Breeze did so, and they strolled down the aisle and out of the doors, where a cocaine white limo was waiting for them at the foot of the steps. The newlyweds were off to board a private jet to Rome for a weeklong honeymoon.

Carter and Mecca watched as they disappeared behind the large double doors of the sanctuary, both of them with smiles on their faces. Mecca looked to Carter and rested his hand on Carter's shoulder.

"That's our baby sister right there. I'm glad to see her happy," Mecca said with deep sincerity.

"Yeah, Zyir's a good dude. I raised that kid. I know that he's one hundred percent . . . no cut. He is going to take care of his family no matter what," Carter stated with a blank expression on his face.

Carter's words were like a dagger straight to Mecca's heart, as Mecca thought about his ultimate betrayal of his own family. He knew at that very moment that he wasn't cut from the same cloth as Zyir or Carter. It was the hurtful truth that he would have to live with for the rest of his life.

"We all we got," Mecca said as he looked into Carter's eyes.

Carter noticed that Mecca's eyes didn't reflect that of a killer's. Mecca looked as vulnerable as a lost young boy, and his words were heartfelt and without prejudice. Mecca truly meant what he had just said. He had made the transformation. Mecca was

ready to leave the gangster life alone and live life without regrets. He hoped that the new country of Brazil could give him
peace of mind and rinse him of the blood that seemed to stain
his hands back in Miami.

The priest walked up to them and prepared to exit the church.
He shook Mecca's hand and then Carter's.

"Thank you, Father," Carter said as he gripped the priest's
hand. The priest exited the church, leaving Mecca and Carter
alone.

Mecca put both of his hands in his pockets and turned on
his heels.

"Excuse me for a second, bro. I have to make a quick phone
call," Mecca said.

Carter nodded his head and watched as Mecca faded into
the back of the church where the dressing room was located.
Carter thought back to the day that he was in the confessional booth and Mecca told on himself. He thought about how
Mecca had killed the only love of his life, Miamor. He also
thought about how Mecca cold-bloodedly killed Monroe.

Carter shook his head, not believing the disloyal acts of
his only remaining brother. Images of Miamor smiling and
in his arms popped into his thoughts, instantly making Carter chuckle while remembering the bond that they once had
shared. He remembered how gangster she was, yet she was so
soft, so ladylike. Miamor was built for a gangster like him, and
Mecca had taken that away from him.

"I love you, Miamor," Carter whispered as he looked to the
head of the church and stared at the cross with a statue of Je-
sus Christ hanging on it. He hoped Miamor heard him from
the depths of the heavens. Little did he know, with Miamor's
resume, she was probably in hell smoking a blunt. That's a
real bitch.

***

Mecca held his cell phone up to his ear, waiting for the person he was calling to answer.

"I'm on my way to the airport now," Leena said as she smiled and made her way through the airport with her son by her side. She wore oversized sunglasses and a wrap over her head to try to disguise herself from any of Estes' goons. Her son had on a baseball cap and heavy clothing, making him chunkier than usual. She was in a rush, trying to get to Mecca, the man she loved, the man who had once almost taken her life. She had snuck away from Estes and was on her way to Brazil to raise her son with Mecca.

Mecca smiled when he heard her voice, and the thought of sharing a life with Leena was inspirational. "Hurry up and get to me, baby," Mecca said, filled with joy.

"I can't wait to see you," Leena said as she gave the flight attendant her boarding passes.

"I can't wait to see you either, beautiful. I am going to make this right, and we are going to be a family. I am going to raise that boy like he is mine and teach him how to be a man . . . a good man. Just like his father was," Mecca said, meaning every word of what he was saying.

"I know you are, Mecca. I know. We are on our way. Mecca Diamond, I love you," Leena said as she boarded the plane.

"I love you more," Mecca said just before he flipped down his cell phone and smiled. "Thank you, Lord," Mecca whispered. He was beginning to believe that there was a God. He was determined to get a better relationship with his Savior and live his life right. He couldn't wait until the rest of his family arrived in Brazil so that his new life could begin. Nevertheless, he would never get to see them.

Mecca heard the sound of a gun being cocked behind him, but he didn't seem startled or even turn around, for that matter. He just took a deep breath and placed his hands together in a praying gesture.

"Our Father, which art in heaven, hallowed be thy name . . ." Mecca said as tears slid down his face. He already knew who was behind him, and it came as no surprise to him.

Carter began to recite the prayer along with his brother as he pointed the gun to the back of Mecca's head.

Mecca had always known that Carter would eventually seek revenge for Miamor's death. He had loved her way too much not to come after him. Mecca's only dilemma had been to figure out when and where Carter would take his life. Mecca was a seasoned street veteran, and the one thing that he knew for sure was that "the eyes don't lie" and on that day, Carter could not hide the hatred he had inside.

Carter knew that if he let Mecca live, Mecca would possibly turn on him one day, just as he did to Monroe. He also felt obligated to avenge Miamor's death, so killing Mecca was inevitable.

Mecca also knew the game. Mecca realized that if he were in Carter's shoes, he would have done the same, so he wasn't mad at Carter for what he was about to do. Once the prayer was over, Mecca stood unflinchingly, with his heart pounding through his chest. There was no malice in his heart, only regret, but he knew that his oldest brother was about to deliver his retribution.

"I love you, Carter," Mecca said as he straightened up his tie and prepared for his death.

"I love you too," Carter replied sincerely as he wrapped his finger around the trigger. "I always will, bro."

Boom!

A single slug went through the back of Mecca's head and clear through his forehead, rocking him to sleep forever at the hands of his own flesh and blood. Karma is real, and The Cartel was no more.

Epilogue

"Diamonds are forever."
–Carter Diamond

Leena covered her ears and took deep breaths as the plane flew through the turbulent skies. She hated to fly, but she hated being apart from Mecca even more. She knew that Estes would be hurt when he read the letter she had written. A single note was all that she had left behind. She knew that he would never understand why she had chosen Mecca over him, but it was something that she had to do. It was a decision that only she would understand.

Her heart jumped out of her chest as the plane dipped violently, almost as if it would fall from the sky. She snuggled her son tightly to her chest and whispered, "Please, God, keep this thing in the air."

The captain turned the seatbelt sign on, only scaring Leena even more. She instinctively reached out to grip the arm of the gentleman sitting next to her.

"Oh, I'm sorry. This flying thing has me kind of shook," she explained in embarrassment.

"It's okay. You're good. The turbulence is really only potholes in the sky. They won't do any real damage. They're just good at causing uneasy passengers a nice scare," he said.

Leena nodded and inhaled deeply to calm her nerves.

"Besides, if you ever want to know if something is wrong,

all you got to do is look at the flight attendants. When they panic, you panic, but until then you're good," he said.

Leena snuck a glance at the stewardess and noticed that she was calm as ever and joking with one of her colleagues. Leena smiled and shook her head in amazement. "Thanks. That actually just gave me peace of mind," she said to the guy beside her.

"No problem. Let me know if you need my arm again, though. I'll be happy to lend it to you," he replied with a smirk and the wink of an eye.

"I'm Leena," she introduced.

"Murder," he replied.

"Wow, that's quite a name," she stated.

Murder smiled, but he didn't reply as he glanced at her sleeping son. The young boy looked like a tiny replica of the very man he wanted to kill. He was definitely a member of the Diamond lineage, a bloodline that Murder planned on destroying.

The funeral service may have been convincing to everyone else, but in the back of Murder's mind, he had known that it was all for show. It was no coincidence that he was on the same plane as Leena. He knew that if he followed her, sooner or later she would lead him to The Cartel, and as he sat next to her his trigger finger began to itch.

"What brings you all the way to Brazil?" Leena asked.

"I have a score to settle with an old friend. Unfinished business."

Breeze boarded the private jet with Zyir behind her. He tapped her lightly on her backside, and she giggled like a schoolgirl as she swatted his hand away.

"I don't know what you acting shy for. I'm about to induct you into this mile high club," he said jokingly. He was completely at ease for the first time in years. There was no business to tend to, no reason to watch his back every second, and no street code to uphold. It was just him and Breeze. Nothing had ever felt so right, and happiness surged through him as he sat next to his wife.

"You're so silly," Breeze said as she leaned into his shoulder and rested her forehead against his. "I can't believe we did it. I can't believe I'm married."

"Do I make you happy?" he asked as he gripped her chin gently.

She nodded. "You know you do," she replied as their tongues met. Finally they were together, and all of the horrible things that had kept them apart for so long no longer mattered. They were soul mates and had weathered the storms that life had thrown their way. Now it was time for their new lives to begin.

"I'm going to go get a few blankets from the flight attendant before we take off," Breeze said. She stood, still dressed in her beautiful white dress, and walked past Zyir.

"Yo, B?" he called after her.

She turned around and was so radiant that his breath caught in his chest. "I love you."

"I know you do, Zyir. You know everything there is to know about me and you still love me. That's why I love you so much," she said. She blew him a quick kiss before walking to the front of the plane.

Zyir closed his eyes in relaxation, but it was soon interrupted when he heard Breeze's blood curdling scream. He jumped from his seat and ran to the front just as Breeze came staggering back down the aisle. A knife was imbedded deeply inside her chest, causing her white dress to slowly turn bloody red as the wound in her chest bled out. Her eyes were open wide in bewilderment, and her hand reached out to Zyir.

"Breeze!" he cried. "No, ma. Not now. Not like this."

She opened her mouth to speak, but choked on her own blood as she fell into his arms.

"Help me! Somebody please!" Zyir gripped the knife and tried to pull it from Breeze's body, but the more he tugged on it, the more blood seeped out.

"No, ma. No. You've got to live," he whispered.

Breeze's eyes spoke to him, telling him all the things that she could not physically say.

"I love you too, ma . . . forever, baby girl," he said to her. "Don't die on me, Breeze. I'ma get you some help." He was too heartbroken to even worry about who had harmed her. He just wanted to get her help and keep the love of his life alive.

He picked her up, scooping her into his arms as she struggled to hold on, but it was no use. His wife died in his arms before he could even step off of the plane. He buried his head in her long hair as he let out a scream of agony.

It wasn't until he heard footsteps in front of him that he looked up.

"Hello, Zyir," Illiana stated with a devious leer as she pointed a gun directly at him.

He instantly regretted leaving his pistol behind. While reveling in his newfound love with Breeze, he had gotten too comfortable, and that mistake had cost him dearly.

As she pulled back the hammer of the pistol and wrapped her finger around the trigger, he didn't even look at her. He focused his attention back on Breeze and hugged her dead body tightly. They had been so close to escaping it all. They had almost had their happy ending, but almost doesn't count. Zyir closed his eyes as he waited for the inevitable shot that would end his life.

***

Carter Diamond, the man who had started it all, sat at the head of the rectangular dining table and smiled as he looked around at his children. His beautiful wife, Taryn, sat directly across from him at the other end. Finally, they were all together again. Heaven had opened its gates for the entire Diamond family, and they all sat amongst a feast fit for kings as they enjoyed this fateful reunion.

Monroe hugged Mecca tightly in forgiveness, as Taryn looked in amazement at Breeze in her beautiful wedding dress. All the while, Carter Diamond presided over them all. He was as distinguished in the afterlife as he had been on Earth, and his heart swelled at the sight of his family. They had been reunited at last. Death had come for them all, and only had one last member to claim.

Young Carter's seat was the only one that sat empty, and although Carter Diamond was proud of his oldest son for surviving in a game where so many had fallen, a part of him still wished that he could be there at this moment. He belonged with his family.

Taryn walked over to her husband's side and kissed his cheek. "He'll be here soon enough," Taryn whispered in his ear. "Let him live his life, and when it is his time, he will fill that seat and our family will be complete."

Carter Diamond nodded and kissed his wife's cheek as he raised his pure gold wine goblet. "To my beautiful wife, twin sons, my dearest Breeze, and to my son who isn't among us just yet. I love you all," he toasted.

They all raised their glasses and drank together as they watched over Young Carter. Through him, the legacy of The Cartel lived on, and it would not end until he had joined them in heaven, where Diamonds lived forever . . .

To the dedicated readers, we love you all.
Thanks for helping us make history.
–*New York Times* bestselling authors,
Ashley and JaQuavis